LONE RUNNER

Borgo Press Books by Ardath Mayhar

The Absolutely Perfect Horse: A Young Adult Novel (with Marylois Dunn)
The Body in the Swamp: An Occult Mystery
Carrots and Miggle: A Novel of East Texas
The Clarrington Heritage
Closely Knit in Scarlatt
Crazy Quilt: The Best Short Stories of Ardath Mayhar
Deadly Memoir
Death in the Square
The Door in the Hill: A Tale of the Turnipins
The Dropouts: A Tale of Growing Up in East Texas
Feud at Sweetwater Creek: A Novel of the Old West
The Fugitives: A Tale of Prehistoric Times
The Heirs of Three Oaks: A Novel of the Old West
High Mountain Winter: A Novel of the Old West
How the Gods Wove in Kyrannon: Tales of the Triple Moons
Hunters of the Plains: A Novel of Prehistoric America
Island in the Lake: A Novel of Native America
Khi to Freedom: A Science Fiction Novel
The Lintons of Skillet Bend: A Novel of East Texas
Lone Runner: A Novel of the Old West
Lords of the Triple Moons: A Science Fantasy Novel: Tales of the Triple Moons
Makra Choria: A Novel of High Fantasy
Medicine Dream: Being the Further Adventures of Burr Henderson
Messengers in White: A Science Fantasy Novel
Monkey Station: A Novel of the Future (Macaque Cycle #1; with Ron Fortier)
People of the Mesa: A Novel of Native America
A Planet Called Heaven: A Science Fiction Novel
Prescription for Danger: A Novel of the Old West
Reflections; & Journey to an Ending: Collected Poems
A Road of Stars: A Fantasy of Life, Death, Love, and Art
Runes of the Lyre: A Science Fantasy Novel
The Saga of Grittel Sundotha: A Science Fantasy Novel
The Seekers of Shar-Nuhn: Tales of the Triple Moons
Shock Treatment: An Account of Granary's War
Slewfoot Sally and the Flying Mule: Tall Tales from Cotton County, Texas
Soul-Singer of Tyrnos: A Fantasy Novel
Strange Doings in the Pine Hills: Stories
Through a Stone Wall: Lessons from Thirty Years of Writing
Timber Pirates: A Novel of East Texas (with Marylois Dunn)
Towers of the Earth: A Novel of Native America
Trail of the Seahawks: A Novel of the Future (Macaque Cycle #2; with R. Fortier)
The Tulpa: A Novel of Fantasy
Two-Moons and the Black Tower: A Novel of Fantasy
Vendetta
Warlock's Gift: Tales of the Triple Moons
The World Ends in Hickory Hollow: A Novel of the Future
A World of Weirdities: Tales to Shiver By

LONE RUNNER

A Novel of the Old West

by

Ardath Mayhar

THE BORGO PRESS

An Imprint of Wildside Press LLC

MMIX

CONTENTS

FOREWORD

Given the same circumstances Katharine Salcomb faced, these would be the decisions I would make. Confident in her strength and capabilities, she chose a hard road, but one preferable to that her cousin would have forced upon her. I wish that more young women would make such decisions, rather than allowing prejudice or expectations of others to shape their lives. We can do anything necessary, when young and strong.

—Ardath Mayhar
Chireno, TX
October 2007

ABOUT THE AUTHOR

The author of sixty-two books, more than forty of them published commercially, **ARDATH MAYHAR** began her career in the early eighties with science fiction novels from Doubleday and TSR. Atheneum published several of her young adult and children's novels. Changing focus, she wrote westerns (as **Frank Cannon**) and mountain man novels (as **John Killdeer**), four prehistoric Indian books under her own name, and historical western ***High Mountain Winter*** under the byline **Frances Hurst**.

Recently she has been working with on-line publishers. ***A Road of Stars*** was her first original novel to appear in print-on-demand format. Many of her out-of-print titles are now available from e-publishers fictionwise.com and renebooks.com; many other novels are being published by the Borgo Press Imprint of Wildside Press and Amazon.com.

Now in her seventies, Mayhar was widowed in 1999, after forty-one years of marriage, and has four grown sons. She now works at home, writing short fiction and nonfiction, and doing book doctoring professionally. Her web pages can be found at:

w2.netdot.com/ardathm/ and
http://ofearna.us/ books/mayhar.html

CHAPTER ONE

JULY, 1864

Katharine paused, her hand on the gatepost, watching the last of the spare horses move away with his new owner up the gritty road in the glare of harsh Wyoming sunlight. She had a bad feeling about this sale—One-Ear Murray was so unpleasant to people that she didn't doubt he'd abuse horses, too. The tales she'd heard about that made her shiver, but there was no alternative. Nobody else had cash money.

The war was still grinding on back East, though nobody here in Wyoming thought it could possibly continue for long, now. It had already devastated the small places along the travel and trade routes, consuming most of the young men and just about all the money. If it went on, 1864 looked likely to be a year of ruin for more people than her own. Even if Pa hadn't been so sick for so long, the situation would have bankrupted the Salcomb Ranch anyway.

This last sale had been her own mount, a yearling she had trained herself.

The thought of a single one of the animals she and her father had raised going into the hands of such a man left her feeling sick.

Almost as sick as Pa, she thought. But that was the reason for this sale, much as she might hate the thought of it. To pay the doctor for his trips out from town was hard enough, but the funeral expense was right there, staring her in the eye. Pa couldn't last long, Doc Edwards said, and she could see it with her own eyes. The funeral, the only thing he asked of her, was not going to be cheap, for people who hadn't had a spare dime in months.

For a heartbeat she longed desperately for her mother, but Ma had been in her grave on Boot Hill for three years now. She might have been able to save Pa, if she'd been here to add her skill with herbs and wild plants to her daughter's efforts—Katharine shook herself and pushed the thought away. Doc said nobody could have saved Pa. His heart was worn out; that was all there was to it.

Behind her she could hear the tapping of her cousin Arnwell's hammer as he mended the porch step. Now that it was certain the bank would take the ranch, he never would have taken the trouble to fix it if he hadn't caught his heel and taken a tumble.

Pa's last fall down the rickety steps never bothered Arnie at all, but now he was, as usual, tending to his own needs. Her cousin was the most self-centered person she had ever known. Ma always said that her nephew only paid attention when his own ox was being gored. How could he have grown up so selfish, after her folks raised him? She never had figured that out.

"Katie!" came her father's weak voice from the bed-room. "Kate?"

It was hard seeing your father become a child, depending on you as if you were his mother, Katharine thought. She climbed the front steps, seldom used since Ma died, and turned into the hot little room where Pa lay dying. He seemed to be afraid when she left him for more than a minute or two. That saddened her. She would have thought, given his long life of lay preaching, and his own daring nature, that he would be ready to meet his Maker, but it didn't seem to help him a bit.

"I'm here, Pa," she said. She bent over the thin shape on the bed, took up the soft cloth she used for washing his face and hands and wrung it out in cool water. Usually he welcomed being cleaned up, but now he was shivering. His blood, she thought, was hardly warming him at all, hot as the day was.

He pushed her hand away. "My feet're cold," he whispered.

She went to the wardrobe and took out one of the thin blankets to spread over his lank frame.

"We sold the last of the stock," she said. "I hated to let Murray have the red yearling, but he was the only buyer Arnie could find. Now we're down to your old gelding Cuss, the mule, and Arnie's Danny. Just enough to get us someplace else, after...after the bank takes over."

He snorted feebly. "After I die, you mean. Comes out to the same damn thing, girl. Put some more cover on. I seem to be gettin' chilled more and more."

She pulled out the wool blanket her grandmother had woven on her own loom back in Pennsylvania. That should melt him down to his toes, she thought, but it didn't seem to help. He reached for her hand as she smoothed the blanket under his chin.

"Stay with me, Kate. Stay with me a while. It makes no difference if you clean or don't clean around here, any more. I need you close by, seems as if. I been pining for your Ma, today. Seems she's right around the corner, waitin' for me. I'm not exactly scared of dyin', you understand, but I feel mortally lonesome. You stay here; it won't be long before I go on to meet her."

He hadn't said so many words all together in weeks. Feeling a shiver of dread, Katharine pulled up her mother's low rocker and sat beside the bed, holding the hand that had been so strong and skilled and that now was withered to frail bones wrapped in a shiny layer of liver-spotted skin.

11

"You're too young to have to go out on your own," Lewis Salcomb murmured. "I wish you and Arnie might've hit it off better—it'd be nice to have you took care of by family, though he's no credit to his folks or us, if truth be told. But you're strong and bright and willing. You'll make it all right enough." She could hear the worry in his voice as he spoke.

"Nineteen—me and your Ma was married when she was nineteen. Maybe you can go to work for Doc Edwards's wife. Or the banker. He needs help with those young'uns of his.

"If folks had any sense they'd hire you to break their horses; you do it without breakin' their spirits. Bein' a woman is goin' to make things hard for you, I'm afraid."

His voice wavered and paused. "Too bad about the war. If it wasn't for that you could go back east to your uncle's family," he whispered.

She squeezed his hand. "You forget, Pa. Uncle Robert's lost all four of his boys already. Aunt Min died last year. There's nobody to go back to. Only Aunt Elsie, out in the Oregon country, is left, and that's a long, hard way to go."

He sighed, and his eyes closed. She could see his heart struggling like some trapped animal beneath his nightshirt. Even as she watched, the frantic motion paused, began again. His fingers squeezed hers with sudden intensity; then his heart halted one more time and was at rest. The hand in hers went slack, and when she dared a glance at his face the eyes were half open, the jaw dropped. Her father was dead, and she could only hope that Ma had been waiting for him.

Katharine rose stiffly, feeling ninety instead of nineteen. She was now an orphan with no money, no ranch, no kin worth shooting at within reach. She pushed the eyelids down over Lewis's eyes, propped his jaw shut with a roll of sheet, and pulled the covers up over his face. Then she

12

moved slowly toward the back door, where Arnwell was still pounding nails into the broken step.

"Pa's dead," she said as she stepped onto the porch. "You hitch up Cuss and your sorrel and we'll take him to town in the wagon. He wanted a real funeral, with the undertaker, the preacher, singing, and all the trimmings, and he's going to get it. Murray just paid me for the yearling, so we have the money—just a little more than enough."

"You're going to waste that on a dead man?" Arnwell sounded angry. "I could get to California on what we got for that horse."

"That was my horse, Arnie. And it's going to pay for Pa's funeral, if I have to beat the tar out of you first."

He might be bigger and stronger than she was, but he'd learned the hard way that determination made up for lack of size. She felt a spurt of fury driving out the numbness that should have been grief but hadn't yet had time to become anything except a vast hollow beneath her breast bone.

Without waiting for her cousin to move, she jumped off the porch and headed for the shed where they kept the wagon. Cuss and Danny were in the pasture beside the lot, and she whistled shrilly to bring the older horse to the gate. Danny followed, and she caught them both and led them into the shed. Backing them up to the wagon, the shaft between them, she began buckling on the straps.

By the time Arnie arrived, she had the wagon ready. "You drive around to the front porch," she told him. "I'll wrap Pa up in the covers, and we can carry him out between us. If the undertaker has to come out here for him, it'll cost more than we have."

Katharine turned toward the house, glad to hide the tears that were now spilling over. Arnie was not somebody she wanted to have to see her cry. But it was hard to go into that room again, where Pa and Ma had spent so many years together and where Pa had been sick for so long.

She could smell a faint hint of urine as she entered, reminding her of harsh realities she had learned about as a child, while helping her mother tend the sick and dying. She drew the heavy blanket off the bed, folding it. She might need that, whatever happened. Then she pulled the light blanket and the worn sheets around the body and secured them with two pieces of rope.

Arnie stomped into the house as if disgusted to have his day interrupted by anything, even death. He started to tug the body off the bed, but Kate's glare stopped him.

"You are going to carry my father respectfully, Arnwell Cobben, if I have to take a gun to you to make you. Now you catch his shoulders, and I'll take his feet. He doesn't weigh anything, any more. That's right."

She found herself wishing she had been bigger, stronger than her light-boned frame allowed. She'd have carried Pa out all by herself, if it had been possible.

It was no great task to carry the long, wasted bundle to the wagon and lay it carefully in the back. Katharine secured the tailgate, for bumping and tossing along the wheel-rutted road might vibrate the body right out the back.

She went into the house again to change her worn pants and shirt for her black skirt and ruffled blouse. It was only fitting that Pa's kin should look decent on such an occasion. Grumbling, Arnie went into the lean-to room that was his and changed his clothing, too.

It was late afternoon, by then, and the sun was almost down to the jagged line of distant mountains. They reached Stony Flat just at dark, and Kate had to go into the hotel and disturb the undertaker at his supper. He came out at once and had Pa's body borne quietly into his place of business.

"With all the frills, plus the choir singing at the graveyard, that's goin' to come to twenty-five dollars," Laz Smith told her, his tone hinting that he thought the price would be beyond her means.

She handed him the three gold Eagles that Murray had paid for her horse. "Keep the change and make sure the grave is kept up," she told him. "We're likely going to have to leave when the bank takes over the ranch. I want his and Ma's graves kept weeded and maybe a flower or two put on them, now and then."

Smith's eyes brightened. "That I can do. With money up front, you're goin' to get a bang-up funeral for Lewis. I've got some black plumes to put on the hearse, too. I'll see to it proper. You want Preacher Elliott to do the service?"

She nodded. He might be a stickler for getting paid, but Lazarus was also a stickler for doing what he was paid to do. Even if she had to leave right now, Pa would get the send-off he wanted, exactly as she had outlined it to the undertaker weeks before, when she first knew for certain that Pa was going to die.

Returning to the hotel, she stepped onto the porch and paused to catch her breath. It had been a strange day, and she felt as if she'd been running for most of it.

As she stood on the porch, just outside the window opening into the lobby, she heard Arnwell's nasal voice. "So it's a deal, then. You'll take her off my hands tomorrow. But I want my money right now. I've got to catch the stagecoach, and I need to pay for my ticket early. Besides, it might be a problem if anybody found out I sold my own cousin."

Katharine stooped and peered at an angle through the dusty window. She could see the back of Arnie's head above the carved head-rest of the sofa. If she'd had Pa's pistol with her, she'd have put a bullet through the back of his skull.

Beyond him, full in the light of the painted oil lamp, sat One-Ear Murray, counting out gold Eagles into Arnie's outstretched hand. She could hear the musical clink as each coin joined those before it. At least he gave Arnie more for her than he'd paid for her horse, she thought with sudden bitter humor.

"Never thought I'd be able to buy me a woman so easy. Not a respectable one, that is. Women don't seem to take to my courting, even here, and it was worse back home in upstate New York. They heard I used to beat my Ma, and it seemed to put them off, somehow, though anybody knows that women need beating regular.

"I appreciate this, Cobben. I've had my eye on that filly for a while now, but she never gave me the time of day. I'll have a great time breaking her to the saddle." That was Murray, all right, just as oily and nasty as ever.

And he was buying her as if she were a horse or a steer. Katharine turned silently and moved to the wagon, where she unhitched Cuss and climbed onto his back. She rode out of town as quietly as possible, but once on the road in the light of the half-moon she kicked the gelding into a gallop. The sooner she got home, the quicker she would be gone. Then Arnwell and Murray could straighten out their soured deal any way they wanted to. She didn't intend to be around to see how it worked out. Knowing Murray, she'd better be well away before he learned she was gone at all.

Returning to the dark house, now empty of everyone who had made it home, was the hardest thing she had ever done. Yet Katharine knew she had to leave long before Arnie came back—if he did come at all. He had flung a bundle into the wagon beside her father's body, before they left the house, and she had not had the energy to wonder what it was. Probably, given what she had learned tonight, that had been what he intended to take with him. She suspected he would stay the night in town and catch the weekly stagecoach, due in the morning. If possible, he'd be well away before Murray suspected his purchase had flown the coop.

She lit the lamp and went through the house, seeking for things she would need to survive in the rough country she intended to cross. Going along the road would be foolish, she knew for certain; that was the first place Murray would look. Even with the war going on, there were enough travelers to spot her and eventually let him know whether she went east or west.

No, she intended to go across country toward the Bighorn Mountains that had notched her western horizon for all of her life. Maybe she could find Rabbit Catcher and the other Shoshone her mother and she had known. The woman had been grateful for Ma's nursing when her baby was sick, and Kate thought she might be glad to help Ma's own child in her time of trouble, despite the growing unease between whites and the tribes. They had come to know that family of Shoshone so well, had grown so close to Rabbit Catcher, that she felt the hostility building between their people and hers might not influence the way the woman would accept her. She had no other option, however, and whatever happened she had to go somewhere.

She took the big blanket, using it to make a pack; into that went a skillet, lead, bullet-mold, wadding, and powder for Pa's old Hawken. She packed all the beans and rice and flour and coffee she found in the kitchen. She packed her winter jacket and the extra pants and shirts Pa would never need again. She added Ma's moccasins, the gift of the Shoshone woman, to the bundle, for her own boots would not last out the journey, she was certain. The big skinning knife from the kitchen she slid into the sheath on the inside of her boot. Pa's work pants fitted her so loosely that nobody would suspect it was there.

She found a length of thong and tied Pa's hatchet to her belt. Better to have basic things attached to her—the world was too dangerous to risk being left without any tool or weapon, and she'd known too many unexpected things to happen to people to leave her survival to luck.

Rolling the bundle tightly, she carried it out and dropped it onto the back porch.

Then she led the Cuss to the shed and saddled him. He didn't like the idea of going out again, after such a long day, and she didn't blame him when he stamped and snorted. Then she left him, going into the fenced lot behind the shed to catch the dozing mule. Sol had been Pa's, not Arnwell Cobben's, and she didn't intend to leave him to her cousin, if he came back here, or the bank either. He'd been her friend for years, since she was tiny and climbed him like a ladder to perch on his broad back. He snorted and stamped as she loaded the pack onto his back and secured it. She put his halter over his head and led him behind Cuss as she heeled the gelding and turned toward the mountains.

The moon was going down in the west when she headed across the dry grit of the plain beyond their narrow strip of river-side grassland. Nobody lived there, though at times different bands of Indians traveled across the dry country. Both air and soil were so arid they sucked the moisture from your body, your mouth, even your eyeballs, but she had crossed it before, and the Indians thought nothing of the trip.

The soil was rocky enough to make it easy to conceal a trail, if she had unlimited time, but now she knew better than to waste her head start. Being clever would come later, when she felt safer. Tonight she would cover ground. Tomorrow she would think about learning to be tricky. Some of the things Rabbit Catcher taught her would come back, she knew. It was certain that Murray, easterner that he was, would find it very hard to track her, though she knew he would put all his energy into trying to find her.

Since he came to Stony Flat, she had seen how tenacious he was. He'd chased a runaway horse once, Pa told her, and shot it when he couldn't catch it. He would follow, she knew for certain, and it was up to her to be smarter, meaner, and more determined than he was.

She kicked Cuss in the ribs and urged him more quickly over the rough terrain. If Arnwell's customer caught up with her, she'd rather be shot like that horse than tied up and taken back to a life with One-Ear Murray.

CHAPTER TWO

When Murray finally went up to his room, Arnie Cobben spent some of his new-found wealth in the bar. Not much—he was too tight-fisted even to treat himself lavishly. Then, listing gently to windward, he went out to retrieve his carpet bag, which he had hidden beneath the seat of the wagon before Katharine came out of the house. He'd added a bundle of extra clothing as a last thought, just before they left. Tomorrow he'd sell the horses and the wagon and add that sum to his nest egg before taking off for California.

When he returned to the wagon, it came as a shock to find Cuss missing. Katharine had suspected something, that was plain, and now it was up to him to hide her flight until he could get out of town. His Danny was dozing between the shafts, but the wagon moved better with a double-hitch. There was a horse hitched farther down the street, sleeping with one hoof cocked and his head down. Arnwell borrowed him, hitching him in place of the gelding, and drove the impromptu team around behind the livery stable, where he backed the wagon into a drooping shed. Returning the borrowed animal to its original place, he climbed onto Danny's bare back and put his belongings before him.

He knew if he remained in town Murray would learn of his loss and demand all that gold back. Arnwell Cobben did not intend to spend the rest of his life mucking out stables or swamping in a bar in Stony Flat, Wyoming. He had the money to leave, and he intended to do just that. He would ride out the west road, find a good spot to camp, and catch the stage in the morning as it headed for its next stop.

He had lived in the same house with Katharine since she was five years old.

He knew that high-headed woman better than he cared to, and he understood that going after her was a waste of time. By now she would be gone, wherever she had decided was best. Catching her was probably impossible, certainly dangerous, and he didn't intend to refund Murray's money. Murray could worry about her—she was no longer Arnie's problem. He'd done his best for her, he congratulated himself. A woman should be bossed by a man, and Murray looked to be one who might even manage to boss Kate.

He wouldn't put it past her to go east to her uncle, war or no war. She was hard-headed enough to do just that, and he pitied any army that got in her way.

Some miles west of Stony Flat he found an outcrop of rock still holding warmth from the day before. There he pillowed his head on his carpet bag, spread his coat over himself, and slept until Danny's stamping woke him just after dawn.

There was nothing to eat, nothing to do but wait, which he did with little patience. By mid-morning, he knew the funeral would be over and the stagecoach should have left town. Murray would know Katharine was gone, and he'd also know that his money was on its way west with Cobben.

Arnie slapped Danny on the rump and sent him galloping away into the prairie. He'd wind up back home, and the bank would get what it could out of him, along with the land and the house. Much good would they do!

Then he heard something that made his heart stutter in

his chest. Someone was pounding down the road at a full gallop. Idiot, he thought. He'll ruin that horse, break his leg or his wind, whichever comes first. Then he had an awful thought. Could it be Murray, searching for him? He'd have had time, by now, to know Katharine wasn't at her father's funeral or at home, and that was a dead give-away.

Arnie crept far back into the tumble of rock, which formed a sort of maze where layers had weathered loose from the original formation and fallen, making jagged angles under which it would be all too easy to find rattle-snakes or scorpions.

Better that than to be caught by One-Ear Murray in his wrath. Arnwell, too, knew about that unlucky runaway horse, as well as several unfortunate Indians, Frenchmen, and unimportant settlers who had gotten crossways with the New Yorker and suffered consequences ranging from painful to fatal.

The horse passed without pausing, and he breathed a sigh of relief. Then he found himself wondering if Murray had already checked the stagecoach, which was already considerably late. Would he return and check the coach again, after Cobben caught it? The vehicle should be along soon, and he had to be out on the road to wave it down.

In fact, it would be best if he was well away from the rock formation, for drivers had learned the hard way about picking up men afoot near any good place of concealment. Too many stages had been robbed by "stranded travelers" with henchmen who were hidden in such places.

Before the stage came, Murray passed again, jogging toward Stony Flat on a heaving horse that dripped with foam. Relieved, Arnie brushed the dust from himself, took up his carpet bag, and walked westward along the road to a spot that lacked even so much as a big rock that might have concealed highwaymen. The sun was mighty hot, but he could live with that.

In a bit the coach came rattling along, the horses fresh from the change at Stony Flat and frustrated at the conservative pace set by the driver. When Cobben waved his hat, the driver pulled up without hesitation. "Sorry we're late," he grunted. "Had to replace an axle before we taken off agin."

"I'm going as far as the coach goes," Arnie told the man. "You want cash in advance?"

"Wait'll we get in. You can settle up at the office there," the whiskery fellow replied. "I can't see anybody makin' a run for it at Snow Creek. There's no place to go."

It was good to get out of the sun, even though the dust was terrible. Arnwell Cobben settled himself beside a heavyset fellow in cavalry uniform, whose crutch said all that was needful about why he wasn't back east taking part in the war. Across from them were a grizzled old man with a scar across his forehead and a dark-skinned youth who looked like a half-breed. The rest of the space was taken up with parcels, and the top of the coach was crowded with boxes with U.S. Army branded into them.

He sighed with relief as he arranged his skinny rump on the hard seat. Murray was headed east, and he was headed west, and wherever his cousin was headed he was glad she was gone. Uncle Lewis hadn't been a bad old fellow but Kate was a ring-tailed terror. He'd tried to pin her down and have fun with her when she was fourteen, and she'd blacked both his eyes and broken his jaw. The only good thing about it was that she never told just what happened.

Arnie still wasn't clear about how she managed to do him that much damage.

He was a foot taller, at the time, and fifty pounds heavier, but somehow she'd twisted out of his grip, grabbed a stick of stove wood, and laid into him like a whole tribe of Indians. There was no mercy in her, he'd learned the hard way. Men he'd fought since he was fully grown hadn't

23

really intended to kill him, and they both knew it. Kate had clearly done her best to kill him, without stopping to think about it. He could outrun her, and that was the only reason he was still among the living.

The thought of her in the hands of One-Ear Murray made him grin. They'd be like two tomcats under a tin tub, and whoever came out in one piece would be a tough nut. Arnie wouldn't have bet on which one that would be, either. One-Ear might be huge, hairy, and built like a bear, but little as she was, Kate could be mean as poison when you riled her. He'd never figured how someone who looked like she did, big-eyed, chestnut-haired, slender as an elf, could pack the wallop she managed. It had to be all those years wrangling horses and handling hay and working around the ranch that made her so much stronger than a woman was supposed to be.

He snickered quietly. Murray was going to hunt her down, he had no doubt at all, but when he caught her he was going to be one surprised Easterner. The man who caught the wildcat wasn't in a bit worse fix than old One-Ear would be when he tried to handle Katharine Salcomb.

* * * * * * *

Ezekiel Murray went to bed as happy as he was capable of being. Although he'd spent more for her than he intended, from the sum gained by selling his dead father's farm back in upper New York State, it left him plenty to get by on until he could set himself up in business or ranching. Getting a respectable woman, a looker to boot, without having to go through all the trouble of courtship and marriage, was something he'd never imagined he could do, even here in this godforsaken country. Now he owned her, lock, stock, and barrel.

Let the Abolitionists back east rave about freeing slaves; he'd always believed that was the best possible way to deal with people. As he had learned young, when he saw Pa whale the tar out of Ma, wives had a strange kind of effect on people's reactions to the way you treated them. The neighbors got really upset when Ma appeared in church with black eyes and bruises.

Slaves didn't count. You could do what you damn well pleased with a slave and nobody could say you nay. The thought of taming Katharine Salcomb sent him to sleep with a smile on his face.

He slept later than he intended. Dressing in his most nearly respectable outfit, he went down in a rush to eat breakfast before the Salcomb funeral. He'd go and show respect. After that was out of the way, he'd grab Katharine and take her the five miles to the cabin he'd bought. That way, nobody would really know what was going on until it was too late to do anything about it. He was a bit wary of her father's friendship with the banker, the doctor, and the preacher. He didn't want any of them interfering, though he knew they would if he gave them the chance.

The hotel clerk assured him that the funeral was set for nine o'clock, a half hour before the stage left town. Murray sauntered out onto the porch, picking his teeth with the gold toothpick he'd won at poker from a gambler back in St. Louis, and gazed up and down the dusty street.

Stony Flat had a principal street, which was the main east-west road, and an alley that went around behind the hotel, the general store, and the livery stable. The café-saloon took up most of the other side of the street, with no alley behind it. Beyond the eastern edge of town the dusty track leading south to north connected far-ranging ranches to the town and the traveled road.

It was a pretty pitiful place, Murray thought. Just right for someone who knew how to get what he wanted. There was no law officer of any kind, and that helped, too. Give him five years and he'd own it, lock, stock, and barrel.

He looked for the Salcomb wagon, but not even a line

of dust interrupted the long double track leading five miles to their river-side ranch. Surely they weren't going to be late to Lewis's funeral.

He dug his father's silver timepiece out of the watch pocket of his vest and stared down at it. Eight forty-five. Already the undertaker's black hearse (which was only a painted wagon) was loaded and ready, the dark horses (not all black, but as nearly as he had been able to arrange) hitched and be-plumed. People had begun moving toward the hillside cemetery, with its straggle of headboards that were already tilting under the attacks of wind and weather.

The preacher came out of his house beyond the church at the crossroad and walked toward the hearse at a solemn pace. Still there was no sign of either Arnwell Cobben—or his cousin, who was Murray's property! Where on earth was she? He hurried over to the undertaker as he came out of his shop and closed the door against the ever-present dust. "You seen the family yet?" he asked Laz.

"No. They are late, but Miss Katharine told me specifically to begin the funeral at nine o'clock, no matter what happened, and that's just what I'm going to do." He turned and gestured to the boy sitting on the wagon seat. Willie clucked, and the horses moved off up the road with the hearse, leaving Murray staring after it. What in tarnation was going on here?

Surely that girl wanted to see her father buried, right and proper? It had seemed so easy when he and Arnwell made the deal—Arnwell! Where was he?

The stage from the east had arrived late the night before with a damaged axle. The passengers were even now eating unusually leisurely breakfasts at the hotel, while repairs were completed and fresh horses were hitched to the vehicle.

Cobben had meant to take that stage west to Snow Creek, he knew. Murray strode across the street and leaned against the wall of the saloon, watching closely. As each passenger arrived, Murray scanned him intently. Cobben wasn't there. A crippled soldier, a scarred old coot, and a half-breed were the only ones scheduled to get into the decrepit coach. Cobben wasn't among them.

Murray turned back toward the hotel, but he went around behind into the alley to the rear of the livery stable. His new horse waited there, and he saddled the gelding quickly and set off southward, toward the Salcomb spread. Something had gone very wrong with this deal; his money had disappeared like dew in the morning.

Nobody cheated Ezekiel Murray. The man who bit off his left ear had learned that, in the course of their conflict. Kerr Clement had sold a much younger Murray a harrow for use on the farm. When he got it home and checked it out there were several teeth missing. Though at the time he was only eighteen, Murray had ridden hell for leather back to the Clement farm, called out Kerr, who was ten years older than he and thirty pounds heavier, and laid into him. Though he lost an ear in the process, Ezekiel had done enough damage to the larger and heavier man to make anyone else in the entire county very cautious in their dealings with him. Now he had to impress that same lesson upon these local fools. What he bought he got, and what he got he held with a death-grip.

He kept the sorrel at a trot, though the horse was heaving by the time he got to the turnoff to the Salcomb house. He could see no sign of life there, but he rode into the front yard and dropped off the horse onto the porch. His steps echoed as he pushed through the front door into the small square of the front room. It felt like an empty house. When he called out, there was only the scuttling of mice to answer him.

When he went out into the back garden, the shed stood empty. No wagon. The lot held no horses—not even the mule was there. Had the two of them conspired to cheat him? He thought about Arnwell—no, that boy had been too anxious to get away to saddle himself with a woman. As for Katharine, she was probably hiding at the doctor's house, and he'd soon have her out of there, whatever it took.

Fuming, One-Ear Murray returned to his mount and rode away, more slowly this time. All the way to town he thought of painful ways to punish the runaway. If he had to shoot her, he could do that, too, but it would have to be done without witnesses. Killing even a slave would be considered murder, out here where nobody had a good idea of priorities.

Unfortunately, killing a woman, slave or not, held penalties not imposed on someone who shot a runaway horse. If he caught up with her cousin, he'd get him, too, of course, but that was not nearly as important as getting his hands on Katharine.

Much to Murray's disgust, nobody in Stony Flat had seen Katharine Salcomb since the evening before. He almost accused the banker of lying, but he thought better of it in time. Bankers were good people to keep on your side of things. The doctor was big enough and tough enough to make even Murray wary about disputing his word, so One-Ear got no joy of him, either.

He changed to a fresh horse and galloped west, hoping to find some trace of Cobben, who just might have ridden away in the night. There was no sign of the wagon or of either horse that had pulled it to town. Cobben wasn't any fool—he'd have known enough not to wait for the stage, and if he could be caught Murray intended to nail him.

The stage was still in front of the hotel, loading luggage and Army supplies. It seemed as if, being late already, the driver didn't worry about how late he would become. In addition to earlier problems, one of the horses had cast a shoe and had to wait to be re-shod. Even if Cobben was waiting beside the road to catch the stage farther along, he'd be able to locate him before the vehicle started out. There was no sign of a rider or a man afoot for miles. As he trotted slowly back toward town, he passed the stage, finally continuing its delayed journey, but he no longer feared that his quarry might escape by that means.

Once in his hotel room, he lay flat on his back and stared at the water-ringed paper of the ceiling. Katharine was not in town. She had not gone east, for several people had ridden in from that direction and none admitted to seeing her. She was not at home; besides which, the bank would take possession of the ranch tomorrow.

She had not departed on the stage. That left one single probability. The fool woman had ridden across country. With the war in the east, it stood to reason that she had headed west. Murray had seen enough of the Wyoming terrain to understand that it was not a good place for those unfamiliar with its dangers. He was going to need a tracker, a scout, who also knew the country and its ways.

With a deep sigh, he closed his dust-reddened eyes. Tomorrow he would hire one. Together they would find his escaped slave and bring her back. Or he would contrive to kill her without letting the guide know. Either way, he would have his due.

CHAPTER THREE

Riding away in twilight, Katharine did not allow herself to think of her father, her home, or anything except the necessity to escape. She had always known her cousin disliked her; the feeling was returned with gusto. But it had never occurred to her that he might sell her. She found it in her heart to regret not killing him when she had had the chance, five years before.

She understood all too well his choice of One-Ear Murray as purchaser. Only Murray, among the local people, lacked the respect for humanity, much less the law, that would allow him to purchase a white woman. Everyone knew he had left the east to avoid the draft—he said so at the top of his voice. His views on slavery were well known to anybody who'd listen. Only he had considerable amounts of ready cash. That was why she had sold the last horses to him, when she would much rather sell them to friends who would treat them well.

Arnwell's need for gold to pay his way to California and to set himself up there was a compelling motive for what he had done, but even more so was Murray's reputation. Arnie would have loved to see her beaten, raped, and abused, and if he wasn't there to see it he'd enjoy thinking about it as he traveled. She knew the sly smirk he had when he plotted something nasty—she should have recognized it after her father died. Her grief had obscured it, she supposed, and now she was paying the price of her negligence.

After the moon set, the pale soil and rock across which she alternately rode and walked glimmered in the starlight. Though it was still early summer, the air was so dry it seemed to suck the moisture from her body, and she had to force herself to wait before touching her water bags. She would need her supply much worse by day, and she had to share it with the two animals as well.

It was necessary to travel as far as possible before sunrise. Keeping the notched peak on the horizon straight ahead, by noon she should find herself intersecting a creek she had visited with Rabbit Catcher when she was a child. If luck was with her, there would still be water there. If not—she didn't falter, but her heart sank at the thought. If not, she had to make it to the foothills before she could be sure of finding enough water for the horse and mule. It was a good two days' (or a good night and day) journey, which would try them to the utmost, if the creek was dry. What she carried would hardly be one good drink apiece for her animals.

Mounting again, Katharine closed her eyes and allowed Cuss to carry on. The gelding had a bad disposition, but when you set him toward a given point he seemed to have an internal compass that kept him on course. She dozed and woke several times before she felt the animal begin to tire. When she dropped onto her feet the sky was beginning to lighten behind her.

She took a long draught from the water bag and poured a double-cupful into her skillet for each of the horses. They snorted, shook their manes, and seemed anxious for more, but she couldn't risk that. If they came to the creek and it held water, she could refill her water bags. If not, this must do them all the way to the foothills, which would be a long, hard way if they had to make it without extra water.

Now the sun was touching the still-white tops of the

distant Bighorns. She lost sight of the mountains as she went up and down the long rolls of land, but somehow their presence was a comfort. Up there were water and wood and small game. If she made it so far, she might well find some trace of Rabbit Catcher and her clan on their regular summer gathering expedition. For many years their band had taken a regular route in summer, and she hoped nothing had changed their habits.

That was a serious consideration, even though the war in the east had allowed tensions to grow between the tribes and the invading whites. Rabbit Catcher was a friend, and she would surely help Katharine hide her trail.

Blessing the poverty that made her father leave Cuss and the mule unshod, the girl knew their hoof-prints would be hard to distinguish from those of unshod Indian ponies, once they were well mixed. Maybe that would work in her favor. Only if Murray had the sense to hire someone who was good tracker would he be able to separate hoof-print from hoof-print.

She checked the position of the sun on the horizon. The season was right. The Shoshone band should be on their way to their usual summer campsites, and Rabbit Catcher had described the shapes of the mountains, the little river that ran down into the plains, and the oddities of rocks and trees so well that Katharine felt she would recognize the proper route, if she got that far.

She mounted Sol in his turn and led Cuss toward the west, checking her route every time they topped a swell and she caught a glimpse of the notched peak. Beneath that, the river ran down from the snows. Surely she could make it so far.

The sun moved higher, burning down blindingly against the pale rock and soil, and Katharine took from her pack the floppy felt hat that had been Lewis's and tied it onto her head with a long scarf. The wind made the brim flap, but the partial relief from glare and the easing of the sun's heat on her face helped.

She stopped reluctantly from time to time, letting the horses crop the scanty grass and the occasional leaves of scrub. Once again she watered the animals. Though her throat longed for a sip even of that flat, warm liquid, she resisted her impulse. She would make it to the creek. There, if no water remained between the shallow banks, she would drink deeply from her own supply and give the horses the rest. Then they would go on to the Bighorns without more.

The plain track left by the horses and her own boots worried her, but speed was more important than hiding her trail, and the wind that constantly swept the plain would obscure the traces in a short time. Once she got up into the foothills it would be easier to hide both her sign and herself.

Though Murray was the worst kind of tenderfoot, still he was farm-bred. It might be that he could track better than she suspected. Or he might hire one of the half-breeds to follow her. She shivered at the thought.

* * * * * * *

Time passed in a dazzle of sun and the grit of pebbles under her boots. The mountains seemed no closer, although just before noon she saw an unsteady shadow quivering in the glare; that was the line of cottonwoods and willows along the creek she remembered. Katharine drew a deep breath of relief.

Now if only there might be water there—from the look of the white peaks beyond there should be a lot of runoff from the snows, even so early in summer.

Surely there would be more than enough to meet her needs. Then she caught the sharp tang of water on the wind.

Cuss raised his head, snorted, and then whinnied

shrilly. Sol had already turned his wise mule gaze toward the almost invisible line of trees and picked up his pace. Soon he outdistanced the gelding, almost running.

Katharine mounted Cuss and gave him his head. Together, the animals made for water, their thirst driving them. When they pushed through the tangle of fallen cottonwood branches and leaning willows to the creek bank, they slowed and she dropped to the ground. The glint of the stream made her heave a huge sigh of relief. There was still water in plenty. This would make the difference, she felt certain, between escape and recapture.

Holding Cuss by the reins, she tied him to a tree trunk to wait while she caught Sol and led him downstream, so he wouldn't foul her own water supply. Being a mule, he wouldn't founder himself by drinking too much, so she left him to it and brought the horse down to drink. Cuss danced into the shallows, splashing rainbows about his hooves. His long, sucking drafts made Katharine long for her own turn, but she couldn't risk having the animal hurt himself. A horse hadn't the judgment of a mule, Pa had always said.

When he had enough for the time being, she tied him again to a tree and moved upstream to the eddy where she intended to refill her water bags and wash her hot, dry face. Her lips tasted salty, and her fingers, when she bathed her eyes, stung them; sweat dried instantly, in this arid climate, leaving only its burden of salt on the skin.

She hung the bulging bags in a tree and waded into the creek, letting it soak her clothing and soothe her skin. Ducking her head, she wet her auburn braid and felt grateful coolness on her neck and back. When she waded out of the creek, she could feel the thirsty air pulling the moisture from clothing, skin, and hair. In ten minutes, she was dry again.

So far, fortune was on her side. What might come behind her was something she refused to consider. Papa always said that a coward feared death ten times a day and wasted all that energy. If you waited until it was the proper time to be afraid, you had a lot more sass left to help you deal with danger and problems.

She rested herself and the animals through the worst heat of the day. Then she watered them again and drank her fill. Last of all, she filled the water bags, and when the sun moved toward the mountains, she saddled Sol, intending to ride him and rest the horse. She caught Cuss, and loaded her pack onto his back.

Refreshed, watered, with enough in reserve, she hoped, to keep them going all the way to the foothills, Katharine set out for the Bighorns and, she hoped devoutly, a meeting with her old Shoshone friend. So far, luck had been on her side. She hoped it would stay there.

Her mount, rested and enthusiastic, stepped out smartly, lost in some mulish meditation. Katharine wondered what mules thought about. She wished she could just move one foot after the other all day long, without having to plan or worry, the way Sol did. Being a mule might be a lot better than being human, though her father always claimed her head was so hard she qualified perfectly well to be one.

She kicked Sol in the ribs and he picked up the pace. The mountains disappeared behind a swell of prairie, only to appear after a while as she topped the next. They were there, near enough to rise above the plain. Tomorrow, she would find herself climbing along the little river that wound through the lower foothills.

It was the right season. Surely she could locate the Shoshone among the hills and join them, for a time. That would, if anything could, hide her tracks from anyone pursuing her.

* * * * * * *

The mountains grew so slowly that she was surprised to realize she was almost there. Now the jagged peaks towered into the sky, their white tops hidden in a light layer of cloud. She could feel them as a weight, a presence looming over her, and the feeling was one almost of fear. She understood now why Rabbit Catcher called them the Great Old Ones.

She found a draw running down from the heights and followed it until she reached a creek that fed into it. Now there was water aplenty, and she drew a deep breath of relief. What lay ahead might be worse than what lay behind, but she was ready, now, to tackle it.

CHAPTER FOUR

Sun-Shot O'Neill was very nearly broke and extremely worried. Both his parents, now old and unable to continue with their mission work to the Plains tribes, were beginning to need care. The church that had sent them out here thirty years ago had promised them that when they grew too old for the work there would be a church home waiting for them, a place built especially for retired ministers of the Faith. The war destroyed any chance of that. Now the home and the church itself had been leveled by cannon fire, as his parents had learned from the few letters that made their way through from the east. The church itself was dying for lack of new members.

Mama was sick, that was the worst of it. She needed to live near a doctor, and Sun-Shot hadn't found a decent scouting job in months. The war had sucked everything, money, troops, and supplies, back east to sustain the fighting, leaving few outside resources for those who remained in Wyoming. His savings were dwindling, and he knew he had to find some kind of work soon, if his folks were to be taken care of.

The Cheyenne among whom he had grown up, knowing them as friends and teachers in his adolescence, had retreated into remote areas and were as poor and desperate as he. They'd trusted his parents, who had doctored them with medicines, and they'd been patient with their attempts to bring them to the Light. He understood, as his people could not, how well the Cheyenne people tended their own spirits with their own religious beliefs. He never talked about it with his mother and father, however, for he knew the truth would hurt them.

The Cheyenne had learned patience in a hard school, but now most whites had become the enemy. Even Sun-Shot was not always sure of a welcome among them. He felt guilty when he visited his old friends, for it was his people and the changes they had made in their world that caused this distress.

He had reached the point when something had to give. He had to find a way to pay future rent on the house he'd located near Stony Flat, as well as for the medicines Mama needed. Only God knew how he was going to manage to do it once he'd gone through the bit of gold left from his last scouting job for the Army.

When One-Ear Murray came looking for him, where he camped along the river, O'Neill found himself wondering quizzically about the sense of humor sometimes shown by Providence. To care for his parents by tracking down a runaway slave seemed ironic, if not downright cynical, given their views on the subject.

"I bought this woman fair and square," Murray insisted. "Before I could take possession, she up and ran away. I can't feel as if she'll get far all alone in this country, but I don't know the trails or the mountains, and I need a good tracker."

Sun-Shot shook his head. "I didn't know there were any black men around here," he said. "And I surely didn't think there was a black woman within a thousand miles."

Murray didn't answer, but that was all right. O'Neill was thinking about how to arrange for his pay. "I'll want money up front," he said to the New Yorker. "I have responsibilities that I have to take care of before I can take off over the horizon. That all right with you? You can deposit two hundred dollars in gold in the bank, so my folks can have money if they need it. Then we'll go. If we find her, that will be my entire pay."

Murray was staring at him as if assessing his worth on the auction block. At last he nodded reluctantly. "I'll do it," he sighed. "Not every man would I trust that way, but the locals tell me you're straight. I don't intend to lose that woman, if I have to drag her back by her hair. So I'll deposit the money, if you'll sign an agreement to lead me to my property or refund whatever's left when we get back, if you should fail."

That was fair. "As long as my folks can draw on what they need while we're gone," he said. "I rent Jameson's old house for five dollars a month, and it won't take much more than that to feed them. What they don't use, I'll refund to you, if we don't catch up with your slave."

Surely there would be a chance to get other employment somewhere along the way, if this didn't work out. Murray didn't look like the answer to prayer, but that was what the unattractive fellow had turned out to be.

"When and where do you want to start out?" he asked Murray.

The man turned his head, his mutilated stump of ear even uglier in the afternoon light. "As soon as I can put the money in the bank; in the morning, at the latest. Meet me there early. We'll get the agreement signed, and then we'll take off. I've got a pretty good idea where to start looking for her trail."

"Not, I take it, along the main road," O'Neill commented.

"This bitch is smarter than she should be." Murray's ear turned red. "She didn't go either way on the road, so she had to take off across country. That's why I needed you."

It took O'Neill a good part of the evening to get his parents moved out of the home of their friend Dr. Edwards and settled in the Jameson house, which was partly furnished. The bed was solid, and there were a table and two chairs. It was no mansion, but it kept the weather out and the rain off. There was even a big stack of wood along the back, left from the last tenants, who had gone back east.

Mrs. Edwards had sent supplies enough for a couple of days, but Sun-Shot knew they would need more soon. "I arranged for a load of groceries to come out by Matheson's boy," he told his mother.

She looked up at him and nodded, but he could see the worry in her eyes. "Are you sure this is honest employment?" she asked in the unfamiliar whisper that was all the voice she had left. "I heard odd things about this man from Doctor Edwards. He sounds very strange and possibly dangerous."

"He is that, but then so am I, Mama," Sun-Shot replied. "I can take care of myself, and I promise not to help him if he's doing something really wrong."

Patrick O'Neill came out of the back room, where he had been stowing their scanty supply of clothing. "God be with you, son," he said, patting Sun-Shot awkwardly. "Come back safely. I don't know how your mother and I could manage without you for very long."

Sun-Shot managed to look confident. "Mrs. Fanning is going to stop in every so often and help with the housework. I traded her my extra pack horse, so she's paid until I get back. She'll cook, too, so you won't have to live off burned beans—I know your cooking, Papa." He grinned at his father, though he knew that their worry would go all the way with him, wherever he wound up.

They were proud people who never let themselves break down. He hugged them both, touching his mother with great care, for she was now so fragile he felt she might break if he held her tightly. Then he turned and left quickly, knowing that if he remained much longer he wouldn't be able to go at all.

These people had given all they had to others for most

of their lives. They'd taught him, along with their red-skinned charges, the value of learning, of honor, and of responsibility. If, for some reason, he could not return—but he shook away the thought and headed for Stony Flat, which was barely visible in the morning light.

One-Ear Murray was already waiting at the door of the bank. Evidently he had rousted out Mr. Donaldsen, who despite being president and chief cook and bottle washer of the bank was a person of almost inhuman patience. The door was unlocked and Donaldsen himself waited inside.

Sun-Shot had an inbuilt aversion to money. That might have been because his parents had always seemed so indifferent to it, and it might have been because of the Cheyennes' contempt for white men who valued yellow metal above honor. Yet now he was obliged to scrounge to make enough to keep his folks alive and as well as possible. It hurt him down deep, but he tried to ignore that.

He signed the papers opening an account, signed the agreement with Murray, which the banker witnessed, and handed Donaldsen the paper with both his parents' signatures on it. He sighed deeply. "I hate to sell my soul for money," he muttered, following Murray out onto the wind-scoured porch. "But I guess I've got to head out with you, now the deal's done."

Murray pointed down the road to the church, where the north-south road crossed the main thoroughfare. "We go south, toward the river."

O'Neill knew everyone who lived within three days' ride of Stony Flat. Down that road lay only the Salcomb horse ranch and, at the very end, Old Man Gossen's shanty.

"Who're we chasing, anyway?" he asked One-Ear. "You said a black woman...."

"No, I said a slave. Which she is. Katharine Salcomb belongs to me. I have a bill of sale from her cousin, who accepted cash money for her person, which he failed to deliver. She has obviously gone across country toward the mountains, and that is where we will go, once we figure out what she took with her. We must search the house to learn that."

How could a man who looked human, though ugly human, think he could buy a white woman? It was more and more certain that even dealing in black people was about to come to a stop, from the rumblings he heard from the few army officers he met. Lincoln was about to make slavery illegal in the South, and before long it would be illegal all over the country.

What on earth had he got himself into? And how could he fulfill his obligation to Murray while keeping his word to his mother?

Finding himself committed to something he knew his mother would abhor, Sun-Shot said nothing to Murray as they rode along the track in the growing heat of the morning. Before the sun was far up, they reached the gray-weathered house and fences and sheds where Lewis Salcomb had gambled and lost at the ranching business.

O'Neill did refuse to enter the house when Murray stepped off his mount onto the porch and pushed open the warped door. "This isn't my house, and I don't go where I've not been invited," he said, but Murray only snorted and tramped into the front room.

When he emerged, face grim, he led the way around to the back, where he stared into the empty barn lot and grunted. "She took the gelding. I had my eye on that one, too. And they had an old mule. Either she took it or her cousin did. The bank's not going to get much out of this lot."

O'Neill ignored him and dropped to his knees to study the mosaic of hoof-prints in the dust. "Unshod, both of 'em," he said. "The mule has a crack in his right front hoof, and the gelding hasn't had his hooves trimmed in a long time. "Won't be too hard to distinguish their tracks from others, if they get mixed. Let me make a cast around toward the west, and maybe I can pick up her trail."

The words almost stuck in his throat. It was wrong to enslave anybody, but a white woman—that was obscene. Yet he thought of his mother, barely able to move about at all, and he swallowed his anger.

He had to follow through, somehow. Maybe, when it came to the crunch, he would know the right thing to do and still be able to care for his kin.

Sure enough, he located the clear tracks of the animals, only slightly filled in by the wind. They headed straight toward the Bighorns, which formed a jagged line against the horizon, and he estimated from the dust the wind had sifted into the tracks that they had been made some time around midnight.

He rose and dusted off his knees. "She's headed west, all right. Looks as if she knows pretty well where she's going, too. That girl was raised here since she was little, they tell me, and her family was friends with Indians. She may know a lot more than you think."

Murray snorted again, louder. "She's a damn female. Doesn't know up from down. My father taught me that, when I was a boy. Women brought sin into the world, O'Neill, and they've done nothing good since. They have to be beaten into shape, that's what my father said, and he proved it with my mother. She never gave up her willfulness, even when he finally beat her to death."

Sun-Shot cringed inside. What sort of demon had he teamed up with, anyway?

CHAPTER FIVE

The hills were covered with grass, green and lush from spring runoff, and tangles of low-growing bushes. Occasional trees rose in folds of land where water collected, and when Katharine reached the bank of the river she was seeking she was glad to see that cottonwoods, willows, and pines grew along its stream.

She could build a fire and cook something at last. Food gave strength, and she had been too worried about Pa to eat much for the past few days. The day before—she thought back, trying to think if she had eaten, and at last she decided she hadn't even nibbled a cold biscuit.

She camped, that night, in a hollow between two ridges, using wood recklessly. She had bathed in the snow water, which froze her blue, and now she intended to sleep warm, as Rabbit Catcher had taught her.

After cooking her meal of flapjacks and coffee, she raked the hot ashes of the fire flat and layered dirt across them. Then she broke off fresh pine branches and laid a thick layer over the warm earth, spreading her blanket over that. She had not built a deep bed of coals, so there wasn't enough heat to kindle the wool.

She had her bed, which would be warmed for a while by the residual heat from her short-lived fire. It wasn't as good as a coal-bed, she knew, but it would let her fall asleep warm. After that, she was so tired she wouldn't know it if she froze, which at this time of year and at night, one could easily do in the Plains. She didn't much care, either. If her life was going to be one constant flight from One-Ear Murray, she'd rather go ahead and die.

Yet she woke the next morning feeling quite well and happy, with her blood singing in her veins. She had eaten well, slept deeply, and this was a fresh day and a new beginning. Today she would go over this first range of hills and begin her climb up the game track at the edge of the river. Once she passed over into the valley beyond the Bighorns, she might find the Shoshone—or someone.

There was still snow up there, but she had her mother's heavy sheepskin cape rolled into her pack, if she should need it. She saddled Cuss, put the heavier pack onto Sol, and led the animals upward as the game trail followed the windings of the stream.

Larger trees now flanked the river, and soon there were spruces among the firs, as she gained altitude. Purple flowers bloomed among their roots, and tufts of bee plant lifted yellow buds. Somehow, their cheerful colors made her feel even more confident.

The climb was steep, and she rested the animals from time to time. Sitting on a rock, she looked back down the folds of steep slopes. Beyond, the plain was a vast dungold sweep. She kept watching for movement out there, though she knew quite well that even if Murray was back there she could never see him in the wide waste of the short grass prairie. She shivered as she turned her steps upward again. She felt, with every instinct man inherited from his primitive ancestors, that pursuit was there— below the horizon, perhaps, but as sure and as persistent as death. Everything she had observed or heard about Murray promised it.

Above her route rose abrupt cliffs of gray rock, weathered into nooks and curves, sometimes broken away to fall at sharp angles, creating tumbles of shattered stone to block the route she wanted to take. The way to the top was longer and harder than she had thought, and she camped twice before leading Cuss and Sol out onto a broad bench of snow lying between a grim gray cliff and a line of tree-tops that obviously marked a drop-off on the other side. It felt, she thought, like standing on the roof of the world, and the clean thinness of the air, the scent of distant snow-fields, was exhilarating.

There was still some distance to go. Beyond the line of treetops a long slope of forest slanted upward still, and she felt certain that was the pass which would lead down into the far valleys she sought. But now the going was easier, the incline less demanding.

Cuss, taking his turn at being ridden, stepped out smartly when she remounted him, and behind them Sol gave a long sigh and picked up his heavy hooves. The smell of clean snow and fir filled her with sudden joy. She was free. She would stay free, Katharine resolved, if she had to dive off one of these cliffs to her death in order to remain so.

Once she joined the Shoshone, if she managed to find them, perhaps she might become one of the tribe—one of the busy wives she had watched when the family camped near the ranch, treating hides, making moccasins, gather-ing plants and berries, and digging roots. It was a thought, though she had no intention of becoming anyone's wife. If she could reach Aunt Elsie in Oregon, she'd heave to and help Uncle Carver farm, tend the children, cut wood—she knew how to do just about everything there was to do around a ranch, and how much different could a farm be?

Heartened, she moved forward over the thick mat of fir needles, between the gray-brown trunks that soared toward the sky, holding pockets of snow in the shadows beneath their dark green crowns. Above her, clouds gathered, drawn by the mountains; occasionally a light sprinkle of snow fell, but so dry was the air that it hardly seemed cold at all. The prickle of ice against her face, stinging her to alertness, only made her feel more hopeful.

They went down into a complex tangle of ridges and arroyos and turned northward to skirt the Bighorn River. There the going was hard, for the erratic track along the edge of the water was broken by falls of rock. Sometimes it edged out into shallows or climbed over piles of boulders that were hard going for the animals.

Yet she followed it, slowly and carefully. An accident here could mean disaster, she knew. Many tribes followed this route, on expeditions of hunting or war, and she didn't want to fall into the hands of the Blackfoot or the Arapaho. After days of travel, she emerged from the deep canyon and gazed out over broken country, spotted with white hills that looked like sand dunes. In the distance the dark line of the Crow Mountains gave her direction. There she would find Rabbit-Catcher's clan, if they gathered there this year. The river now ran between shallow banks, and there was plenty of willow and cottonwood to provide fire, if she dared use it. Yet Katharine had learned a lot from her Shoshone friend. Fire, here in the mountains, could bring unwelcome visitors, she knew, and she slept without it and ate raw bacon and cold flour paste as she traveled.

* * * * * * *

She found a place where the river spread out and was shallow enough to risk swimming the horses across. Beyond it, looming large now, were the mountains she sought. The long dark shape of them was somehow chilling, yet once within the trees skirting the lower slopes of the Absarokas, Katharine found a sheltered spot behind a split of fallen stone and built a fire at last.

The animals huddled close, for at those altitudes night brought even worse cold. She and the animals had been soaked in snow water, dried while moving, and now needed to warm themselves. Katharine was starved again for cooked food, as well, and she fried a skillet of bacon, frittered flapjacks in the leftover grease, and felt the heavy food fill her with new energy.

After covering the fire thoroughly, she led her animals away into the twilight, moving a long way before settling for the night. Anyone attracted by smoke or cooking scents would investigate, and she wanted to be well clear of the site before falling asleep. She found a spot at last, tucked behind a knee of stone and covered by the branches of big fir trees. Full and relaxed, she lay for a while in her blankets, staring up through a lace of pine and fir boughs into the starry blackness. Now the reality of her losses hit her with devastating suddenness.

Five years before, she had possessed mother, father, and ranch. She had begun working with the horses, discovering her talent for taming unbroken colts and training them to the saddle. The future had looked promising, and, being so young, she had never expected anything to change.

Now she was alone, except for distant kindred who might or might not welcome her into their family. The ranch had fallen victim to the expenses of her mother's and then her father's last illnesses. Her cousin had proven to be a scurvy bastard. Except for the horse and the mule and her scanty supplies, she was without possessions and alone, adrift in this endless country.

A few tears trickled into her ears, and she turned on her side and blew her nose noisily. She had no time for self-pity. Tomorrow she must climb into these dark-forested mountains and find her Shoshone friend. Her care in trying to hide her trail might or might not help her, depending on the competence of the guide Murray might hire.

Katharine wiped her face and pulled her blanket around her ears. She closed her eyes with determination, and so weary was she after her day's exertions that sleep overtook her almost instantly.

* * * * * * *

She woke in the first light of dawn to a feeling that she was being watched. In the night she had turned onto her other side, and now she opened one eye a slit and peered out beneath a fold of the blanket. She could see a tangle of mountain mahogany, behind which Sol's dark rump was just visible.

As quietly as possible, she slipped the blanket back and sat, turning to look about her. The thick fir trunk beside which she had slept gave her a solid barrier at her back as she examined everything within range.

The gray ledge of rock forming a sort of terrace along the slope was covered with fir needles, now dotted with horse dung. Beyond the tiny clearing in the nook was another thicket of mahogany bushes, in which two small birds were sitting. Beneath the lower bush, half hidden by a spray of leaves, was a pair of berry-bright eyes. A dark oval face became visible around them, and then she realized that a small boy was hidden there, staring at her as intently as she stared at him. Her heart sped up, but she kept her expression calm and pleasant.

"Greeting to you, my small friend," she said, using the Shoshone words she had learned from Rabbit Catcher. If this were a Crow she would be in trouble, given the hostility between the tribes, but she could only hope.

The child slid out from under the bush cautiously and sat cross-legged, facing her. But when he spoke, her small store of Shoshone could not keep up with his words.

She raised her hands, palms out. "I am sorry. I speak only English well. Do you know Rabbit Catcher of the Three-Peaks Shoshone?" she asked in her own language.

He studied her carefully. Then he made the sign for wait and slipped backward out of sight.

"He might be bringing warriors to kill me," she said to Sol, who stuck his nose out of the mahoganies at her other side. "But he didn't look upset. Maybe he'll bring someone who speaks English, if nothing else."

The mule flopped his ears forward and snorted. Beyond him, Cuss, who had been hobbled, stamped and snorted, too. But though it was now daylight, Katharine did not load up her belongings. The boy had said to wait, and she had a feeling it might serve her well to obey his signal.

The sun rose above the mountains to the east, lighting the treetops. Katharine climbed a bit higher up the slope, leading her animals to a patch of grass, where they began grazing. One did not waste such a chance to rest and eat, so she took out a pone of hard bread left from her cooking earlier, and nibbled it as she waited.

When Sol raised his head and snuffled and Cuss stamped and whickered, she knew someone was coming. She crawled into a clump of bushes and watched the ledge below, where a well-used game trail ran.

In time, the child she had seen earlier came running along it, checked when he found her camp site empty, then spotted her upward trail and came toward her. Behind him were three women dressed in deerskin tunics.

The tall one was a stranger, but she recognized another as Mourning Dove, who had come once to her mother's house while Rabbit Catcher's son was ill. What luck to find someone she knew, here in the mountains! Dove spoke a bit of English, enough to go on with until Katharine could learn more Shoshone.

She rose and moved slowly downhill to meet the group. The third woman was very old, and she stared hard at Katharine when they met. Katharine gazed back, hoping the ancient would find no bad omen in her. She needed the help of these people, if she was to escape westward and find her aunt's family.

She extended her hands to the old one, who took them and bared her gums in a face-shattering smile. She looked like an ancient baby, wrinkled and worn, yet holding in her faded eyes an irrepressible spark of youth and laughter.

Katharine smiled, too, hoping that this meant her acceptance into the gathering band. Perhaps, when they found the larger group, her old friend would be with them, as well. The tall woman gestured, and the Indians turned back the way they had come. Katharine hastened to bring the horse and mule, and together they moved along the trail together, the women chattering so fast the girl caught only a word here and there.

She laughed, just the same. Having human company was wonderful, after so long spent with nothing to talk to except the animals.

The boy strayed behind then, clearing away all trace of horse droppings, then slipped up beside her, saying nothing, and matched his steps to hers. Could this be Rabbit Catcher's son? Something in his regard made her feel he might be, for there seemed to be recognition in his enigmatic gaze.

Even if he were not, she felt no hostility in this group. Whatever the problems between white and red in these troubled times, they seemed not to extend to her. For that she was most grateful.

CHAPTER SIX

Sun-Shot stared across the glare of the plain toward the jagged line of mountains. There was no sign, now, of the tracks that had been so easy to follow when he and One-Ear Murray angled away from the Salcomb ranch. Once that girl left the creek, which had obviously been her goal from the beginning, she had taken a lot of trouble to stick to rocky ground and to check her back trail for signs of her passing. It was taking far longer than it should to pick up a scuff-mark here or a colorless crumb of horse-dung there. Murray was definitely not happy, although O'Neill was beginning to take grim delight in the ability of his quarry.

"Just one damn woman oughtn't to be this hard to trail," Murray kept complaining. "Women can't find their way back from the privy, my Daddy used to tell me. What's wrong with you, O'Neill? You act like you don't want to catch up with her."

"Your daddy didn't know what he was talking about," Sun-Shot finally allowed himself to reply. "He didn't know any Indian women, that's for sure. I used to know a Cheyenne girl who could out-track, out-fight, and out-run just about any man in her village, and a white man didn't stand a chance.

"Your daddy certainly didn't know the sort of white women I've known, either. My mother used to travel by herself from village to village with medicine, when there

52

was sickness in the tribes, and she never got lost or had a problem that she ever mentioned. Sounds to me like that man was so set on his wrong-headed views that he couldn't see what was in front of his eyes."

Sun-Shot dropped from his mount and studied a patch of gravelly soil, considering if the depression there was made by a horse's hoof or that of a stray buffalo, but the wind had drifted dust into the contours and it was impossible to tell. He sighed and rose, brushing grit from his knees.

"I think she's making straight for the Bighorns, like I said from the first," he said to Murray. "And you're right—I'm not happy about catching her for you. No white woman, or any other kind, should be a slave. My folks don't believe in slavery. Still, if I'm to earn the money you put up, I've got to do the job.

"I suggest we go as fast as possible to the foothills and then search along the edge of the range for some trace where she might have passed. We're a couple of days behind her already, what with starting late and looking under every bit of brush and behind every rock.

"You hired me to track, and if you're going to keep on telling me how to do the job you might as well do it all by yourself." He knew an edge of irritation was in his voice, but with a bastard like Murray it was impossible to control his dislike completely.

Murray looked down from his saddle, his wide hat shadowing his face. The malign gleam of his eyes sparked beneath the brim, and Sun-Shot felt a shudder go over him. This was a strange and uncomfortable employer, and the sooner he finished this task and left him behind, the better he knew he would feel. The man made you feel as if you needed to keep your back to a wall.

"Then do your goddamn job and get us on the trail again. This messing around in the brush is wasting time," Murray growled.

Sun-Shot climbed onto Goldie and kicked him into motion. Instead of looking at the ground, he set his gaze upon the tallest of the peaks on the horizon and headed in that direction. Behind him his pack horse snuffled and Murray's animals snorted as dust, kicked up by the constant wind, swirled into their noses.

He knew how they felt. His own eyes gritted when he blinked, and there was a fine crunch of grit between his teeth. He would have sighed, but it would have let dust go down his gullet, too, and he had enough problems without that.

* * * * * * *

Two days later they reached the foothills. Now Sun-Shot had to earn his keep, or he knew Murray would be demanding his money back. While Murray grumbled at the delay, Sun-Shot set up a decent camp, dug a latrine, as he had learned to do while scouting for the Army, and found good patches of grass for the horses.

It was plain the New Yorker hadn't the faintest notion about living on his own in this country, for he continually bitched and groaned and mumbled curses. At last Sun-Shot could stand it no longer.

"I was raised by decent people," he told Murray. "They didn't talk that way. *I* don't talk that way. If you can't open your mouth without cursing, just keep it shut or I'll shut it for you." His glare seemed to get his point across, for Murray subsided to an occasional "Damn!"

It was strange the way white men cursed, O'Neill thought. The Cheyenne knew how to do the job right. They started with your most remote ancestors, picked up your least desirable kin, came down to your personal looks and failings, and then called you something that came out as "cowardly shit-eating coyote" or the equivalent, however they phrased it. For cursing inventively, he'd take a

Cheyenne, every time.

They seldom repeated themselves or copied from each other, for insult was a fine art in the clan of the People he knew. White men just repeated the same tired old insults until it got plumb wearisome.

Having shut off the cursing to some degree, he felt a bit better as he took up the task of tracking northward along the toes of the Bighorns. Grass was growing quickly, spurred by snowmelt water and the warmth of early summer; it concealed tracks better than the best trickery could. He wasted no time in beginning his painstaking search of the terrain.

There were several streams that came down from the heights, each cutting a deep canyon into the rocky flanks of the Bighorns. He searched the approaches to each, along with the trails that game had cut beside the water on the way up into the heights above. Not until he reached Crazy Woman Creek did he find anything promising, and by that time he and Murray had moved their camp three times.

This young woman was no fool. Her direction had seemed to head toward the southern end of the range, but as she traveled she'd evidently angled northward toward some spot she had in mind all the time. It was as if she knew something he didn't and was heading toward a predetermined meeting. If that happened to be with some group of Indians who ranged this area, it meant his job was going to be a lot harder than he had thought.

When he met Murray at their latest camp, the New Yorker was disgusted and surly. "Might as well hand me back my cash," he grumbled as Sun-Shot rode into view. "I could've done as well all by myself. Anybody can lose a trail." He spat into the dirt at his feet and glared up as O'Neill dismounted and stood over his employer. "Don't think you're going to give me any excuses, either. You've lost her, and that's plain as pie."

This was really a nasty man, Sun-Shot thought, but he kept his temper under control. "You would never have made it this far," he said, "if I hadn't kept you from running off on tangents every few miles. You can't tell a mule's sign from a rabbit track."

He managed to grin, though a bit sourly. "Besides which, I think I've found where she crossed the Bighorns. At least, I think she started up the canyon trail beside Crazy Woman Creek."

Murray did nothing to help with building a cook-fire or with cooking, either. He seemed to think O'Neill was a temporary substitute for his escaped slave, which didn't make Sun-Shot like him any better.

For that reason, he had never taken any trouble about cooking for his employer. Anything that didn't bite back was fine with O'Neill, so he'd heated canned beans and made pots of coffee all the way across western Wyoming. If he fried bacon, he'd have to clean the skillet, and Murray's appetite, by now, was too unimportant to justify the extra trouble.

They ate in silence, and Sun-Shot swilled out the coffee pot in the creek beside which they were camped. He rolled himself into his blanket gratefully, feeling the long miles of riding as a weariness in his bones. Murray, who had ranged nearer the camp, seemed exhausted, too, and Sun-Shot wondered what the big man had found to do to get so tired.

He slept, as usual, with one ear cocked and one eye open. He had learned the trick from his Cheyenne brothers, long ago, and it had saved his life more than once. When he heard a gasp in the middle of the night, he woke instantly, alert for more sounds.

What he heard was a whisper—a mere breath carrying Murray's word, "Snake."

This was not a new problem. More than one sleeper had waked to find a rattlesnake sharing his blankets and his body-heat. The thought that Murray was suffering this initiation into the ways of the West was truly satisfying, Sun-Shot thought, as he eased out of his own blanket and crept toward the sound of wheezing breath and chattering teeth. If the fool got bitten, it wouldn't really make him unhappy at all.

He'd noted the direction of Murray's head before he fell asleep, so he made for that end. When he was within whispering range, he asked, "Where?" the sound of his word barely audible.

"Belly," came the agonized reply.

That was good. If the reptile was right up at the man's face, they stood a good chance of getting him bitten in a spot that would kill him quickly. Hampered by the blanket, however, the snake was less likely to be able to coil and strike.

"You be still as death," Sun-Shot breathed. "I'm going to wrap him up in the blanket and jerk him off you."

Only the presence of death on his stomach kept the man from protesting, Sun-Shot knew. He'd protested everything, all the way they'd come, from where and when to camp at night to how to build a fire to the best way to saddle a horse.

Now O'Neill rose to his knees and leaned forward, spacing his hands over the dim lump that was Murray's body. Then he grabbed with all his might, bundling the squirming shape beneath the blanket into a wad and snatching it free of the shivering man.

He jumped up and carried the mess to the ravine down which the creek ran. Then, working one edge of the blanket free, he shook it over the chasm like a housewife shaking a rug. There was the sound of something thrashing through the alders below, followed by a dim thud.

Then a storm of rattling shook the very air. That was one angry rattlesnake down there, he thought, grateful that it was no closer.

"You didn't kill it!" Murray griped, as Sun-Shot returned from his errand. "Why in hell didn't you kill that
thing?"

"You want me to go down and get it and bring it back
so you can do the job right?" he asked.

That silenced Murray. Sun-Shot handed his employer
his blanket and turned back to his own sleeping place.

He didn't know if Murray slept or not, but he rested
well, himself. Only when a magpie called shrilly in the alders did Sun-Shot open his eyes to find that the east was
touched with gray.

"Time to rise and shine." he called.

For once, Murray said nothing; without protest he saddled his own mount and helped Sun-Shot load the pack-
horse. They rode together along the toes of the mountain
range, and it was at least two hours before Murray began
to talk again.

If this was the effect a rattler had on his employer,
Sun-Shot thought, he maybe ought to catch a few and
carry them along in a bag. Anything that would silence
One-Ear Murray had to be more valuable than he'd ever
believed a rattler could be. But he said nothing. He'd had a
respite, and that was something to be grateful for.

Crazy Woman Creek proved to be the route she'd
taken. Not that she was careless, but here there were
patches of damp from the melting snows above; there was
also a lot of rock that showed the tiny marks of passing
hooves. There wasn't much way you could erase a scrape
on granite.

He found the site of her camp before nightfall, noting
with approval the care with which she had removed her
traces. "I think she made her bed over the coals of her fire.
Smart work. She must have learned a lot from those Indians," he observed to Murray as they looked about the area.

"I don't see a thing," One-Ear said, staring at the
ground, the surrounding growth, and the neatly concealed

site of the fire. "You're bullshitting me, O'Neill. This doesn't look a bit different from any other place we've crossed."

"That's why you're paying me those gold Eagles," Sun-Shot grunted. "You wouldn't have had any notion which way to set out, in the beginning, if you hadn't had me along. Take my word, which you're paying for in good gold coin. She went up this way, and she'll go down the other side by a route I know like the back of my hand.

"After that I don't know. Depends on whether she knows where she's trying to go or is just running." He sighed, thinking how he would have felt as a youngster, left without any family or job, with no place much to go and running from a bastard like Murray.

She was taking her time now, he found as they climbed. There was no horse dung to be found on the trail, which meant she must be listening for the sound and stopping when one of them fouled the track. Probably she was brushing it off into the bushes with a branch of fir, but it was hard to tell because the wind kept scouring all the marks from the ground.

If it hadn't been for Murray, Sun-Shot would have enjoyed the trip up the canyon. In early summer everything was greening or blooming, insects skittered out of his way, and the air smelled clean and fresh. It was Murray's constant griping that got him down, and as they broke camp one morning he finally spoke up.

"Are you going to get ready?" O'Neill asked with exaggerated patience, "or do you just want to forget the whole thing and go home again?"

Murray grunted and heaved himself into his saddle again, as the guide led his own mount up the narrow path beside the creek. "You'll have to walk before long," Sun-Shot called back over his shoulder. "If this track is like others I know, it'll get narrower as it goes higher."

Before they'd gone a half mile, he found he'd been

correct. At one spot a pointed boulder thrust out of the canyon wall directly over the path. A horse could barely make it under, and a man had to stoop, even afoot.

Grumbling still more, Murray got off his mount and crept through the opening, avoiding any glance down the steep incline toward the creek below. Sun-Shot noted with amusement that every time a rock rolled away beneath hoof or foot, Murray flinched and hugged the wall beside him more closely.

They kept climbing, as the path twisted to follow the meanderings of the canyon. Now it was so narrow that he rearranged the loads on the horses, to keep the width of packs from pushing the beasts off the edge. Then, with Murray using more of his purple language, O'Neill removed the biggest of the beasts' burdens and loaded them onto himself and his employer.

"I am no damned mule!" Murray protested, as Sun-Shot prodded him up the trail. "I'm paying you, after all. You ought to carry whatever needs to be taken uphill."

"So I'd be all loaded down, when you finally fall over the edge, and wouldn't be able to catch you and haul you back up again," O'Neill began. Then he paused, listening.

"What the hell is the matter now?" Murray asked, turning carefully to look back.

"Keep your mouth shut. I think we have company," the guide told him. Sun-Shot reached back to touch the lead horse reassuringly, hoping that the person or animal on top of the cliff above them wouldn't cause the animals to whinny. That would be a dead giveaway.

"Move slowly and carefully," he whispered to Murray. "Anybody overhead can't see us. The canyon wall's too steep. If we make no noise, maybe we can slip past without their being any the wiser."

Even as he spoke, he heard an elk bugle. That would divert the attention of hunters, if there were any up there, from whatever might be going on down in the canyon. He pushed against Murray's bundle. "Get a move on while we have the chance," he said in a stage whisper.

For once, Murray didn't argue but got a move on; they covered a considerable distance before Sun-Shot called a halt again to listen for any activity in the forest above. It seemed like days instead of hours before they cleared that loop of the path and found a smaller stream coming down from the right to join the bigger one that now was a half-mile below them.

After that, Murray was quieter. While O'Neill's advice hadn't got through to him, the danger of hostile Indians on this vulnerable path seemed to have done the job.

* * * * * * *

They came down the western side of the Bighorns three days later, and Sun-Shot pointed toward the river canyon below. "She'll either go upriver or down. Like I said, it depends on what she's after. There's no white people living in this area, though quite a few travel through here."

Murray simply grunted and kicked his horse into motion. The rocky trail along the river showed no sign at all, and O'Neill decided to camp downwind of a pile of boulders while they decided which way to investigate.

"You're wasting time again," Murray observed. "I can always tell."

"Let me give you an idea of what we have to do," O'Neill said. "There are two directions, surely you can see that. Here you can't cross the river—look at those cliffs beyond it. I couldn't climb them, and nobody on earth could get a horse up them, if we could get across the water here alive. Which, by the way, is unlikely. She had to go this way"— he pointed—"or that way.

"It'll take more time than we should spare for me to go both ways. Why don't you take one direction while I ride along the other? That way we'll cover it in half the time."

His employer grunted sulkily, but it was evident that he saw the logic in Sun-Shot's words. "All right. Soon as the sun's up, I'll go north, you go south. I think I got a pretty good idea what to look for, after watching you for so long."

He was right, for before noon the next day Sun-Shot heard two shots, the agreed signal when one of them found a trace of their prey. Despite himself he felt a quiet pride as Murray pointed out a pair of tumble-bugs slowly trundling a ball of horse manure along beside the trail.

"That's nice work, Murray," he told the man. "I didn't think you had it in you."

They chewed jerky as they rode, now, and in three days they rode out of the river canyon and saw the spot where she must have crossed it.

"Seems as if she's heading toward the Absarokas," Sun-Shot said, staring at the long line of dark mountains lying beyond the valley.

Murray looked, too, frowning as he saw the shadowed peaks, the abrupt gray heights that rose, seemingly without access, through the thick fur of forest to thrust gray peaks into the sky. "Rough country. How can a woman...?" He paused and looked sideways at Sun-Shot. "How can anybody find a way through that?"

"You watch. She will, and we will, too, though I'd give a lot to know why she picked that way and not the easier trail to pick up the Wind River to the south. Could be...." He didn't finish the sentence aloud, though he was thinking, Could be she knows somebody who might be up there.

They spent a long, hard day and a half crossing to the mountains. There, once again, they parted, searching along the feet of the heights for some trace of her passing.

Again Sun-Shot nodded, realizing that she had sense enough not to stick to one of the creeks crossing the plain.

That would make trailing her entirely too easy. Evidently she carried enough water to see her and her animals across. That probably meant she wouldn't climb the range along one of the big creek canyons.

They searched for days before they found where she climbed the foothills along a small creek still full of snow water. The trail was dim, traces of her passing almost impossible to find now, for they were at least four—maybe five days or a week behind her.

They came suddenly upon clear sign—nibbled leaves and grass still showing the more than overnight presence of horses. Not her usual style, Sun-Shot knew, and wondered why she had changed her technique.

"Now this is downright strange," he said, examining the ground. "Far as I can tell, that woman and that horse and that mule should still be right here. There are damn sure no tracks leading off in any direction."

He cast uphill and down, following the granite ledge for some distance without finding anything except bird tracks in occasional patches of dust. The sun went over the mountain, and shadows began creeping beneath the trees, but he had no more idea where their quarry went than did the hawk quartering the sky above him. Hell, the hawk probably knew exactly where she was.

"I'll be damned if I can tell where she went," he admitted at last, his tone rueful. "If I had to guess, I'd say she met up with a band of Indians and they took over the job of hiding her trail."

"So what do we do now?" Murray asked. He wiped his chin with his sleeve, for he had taken the opportunity to eat again. "You seem to think that damn female can work magic. I think you're just fooling around, trying to get my money without doing the job I hired you for."

Sun-Shot wondered if he could ever square his conscience if he shot the man between the eyes, right this minute. Then he thought of his folks and regretfully discarded the thought.

"You may be a thief, Murray," he said. "I'm not. You're just going to have to realize that this is a bigger job than either of us thought it would be. Tomorrow we might as well head west, over the mountains. If she goes on the way she started, west is the way she chose and she's sticking to it."

But as he dropped off to sleep, Sun-Shot O'Neill was smiling. He'd tracked horse thieves, deserters, bank robbers. But this was a fugitive worthy of his skills. He hated to think about catching up with her and turning her over to that bastard Murray. That would be a pure-dee shame, and no joke.

CHAPTER SEVEN

Although Katharine thought she knew something about the Shoshone, she realized very soon that she had seen only a hint of their lives. What Rabbit Catcher had taught her, while she and her son stayed at the Salcomb ranch, had been valuable, so far, but she quickly learned more.

Now the girl watched the children remove any trace of the passing of her animals and so many people; she realized she must pay attention, for as hard as she had worked on her way to that point, she knew she had neglected things these small ones would not have missed. Behind their line of march the children brushed the tracks away with clumps of twigs and then stamped in three-toed bird tracks, using twigs to make the marks. Surely, she thought, they could not afford the time to accomplish this painstaking concealment every time they moved across country. When they stopped to gather buds and roots in a damp cup between boulders, she asked Dove the question.

The woman looked amused. "Where one white go, others come. We see this all-time. You white. Other will come, so we hide track. Not want to fight white men. Not many warriors with us now; while we find seeds and plants, they go hunt for meat."

"You are right, you know," Katharine said. "I am running away from a white man, and it will surprise me if he doesn't hunt me, tracking me across the country like a wolf."

Dove shrugged. "You want him catch? Or not want him catch?"

It was a fair question; Katharine sat to clean dirt from her pile of roots while explaining. "He bought me from my kinsman. He is cruel, dirty, and dangerous. I do not want to live with him, so I left. I have kindred in the Oregon country, and I must try to go there."

"Ah." Mourning Dove gathered their combined root-piles into a basket and rose. "My people not sell daughter to bad man. Whites different."

And that was for damn sure, Katharine thought, falling into line with the others and trudging along toward whatever goal they had set for themselves. The moccasins she had donned were easier on her feet than the boots that now rested in her pack, and their tracks would be harder to distinguish from other moccasin prints.

Sol and Cuss went on ahead, their marks obliterated by those following them, while the children remained behind, their sharp black eyes catching and removing any trace of human or beast. Katharine grinned, thinking that if anybody tracked her so far, he would be mighty confused to find her camp, clear and plain, and no trail leading away from it.

For the first time in many days, Katharine felt safe, though she knew that if Murray and whatever help he might bring came upon their group he would shoot all of them. He had a reputation for hating Indians and abusing any who came into his hands. She couldn't stay with these people for long, for she could never live with herself if she brought disaster upon them.

What would happen to her didn't bear thinking about. She had known women who were raped; most survived and went on with their lives, but the beatings and tortures such a madman as Murray might inflict on his slave would probably break her spirit, possibly even her mind. Almost certainly he would cripple her body.

No, if there should be a real danger of capture, she must kill herself, if she had to leap off a cliff or cut her own throat. She would not become the property of One-Ear Murray.

Her boot-knife fitted into the loop at her belt, and now she fingered its bone handle. It would do, lacking anything better.

They moved more swiftly after leaving the side of the mountain. Now they angled through the foothills and approached the small river between the ranges, finding an array of plants that Katharine had never suspected of being edible. Seeds from careless weed, stalks of saltbrush, roots of thistles and lilies and flowering plants she had never seen went into the baskets and bags, some to be eaten immediately, some to be dried and stored for winter. She noted every edible plant harvested by Dove and her group, feeling that this knowledge might save her life, before she was done.

In two days the group joined a larger one, where the hunters waited. Rabbit Catcher was there, and when Katharine explained her predicament the woman nodded gravely.

"We take you west, beyond mountain. You have horse, mule, so you go fast. I know that man Murray. He do bad thing to Lakota he catch. I know, I hear from people beyond mountains. He not one to be with. We go tomorrow."

Katharine shivered. She had almost allowed herself to forget the threat hanging over her. Now she could hardly wait to set out with Rabbit Catcher and Dove.

There seemed to be no objection from the Shoshone to having part of their band set off on their own. This was evidently a normal part of the gathering process, allowing relatively small parties to cover a lot of territory, for even with the summer spurt of growth, patches of the different food plants were often small, and good gathering places were far apart.

When Katharine rode out of the camp after Rabbit Catcher, they were accompanied by Dove, by Owlet, the boy who had found her, and by three other women and their children. They took more horses now, for they headed back east to the valley, intending to go around the foot of the Absarokas and up the Wind River. They would need pack animals to bring back the roots and seeds and plants they intended to harvest.

Katharine felt a bit uncomfortable about retracing her steps, but with other unshod horses along she knew it would be hard to distinguish the tracks of Cuss and Sol from the rest. She only hoped that One-Ear had taken his loss sensibly. If not, she hoped even more devoutly that he had not found one of the best of the local trackers as a guide, if he'd decided to pursue her.

It was a long, leisurely trek, for the gatherers paused for days at a time when they found good sources of food. Cattail roots and shoots were fairly easy to harvest, but she found Dove's method of getting arrowhead tubers fascinating.

The woman would wade out into shallows of the small river up which they were traveling, towing a basket behind her. She would root vigorously with her toes, digging up the white egg shapes, which floated to the surface.

Katharine soon waded in after her to catch the floating tubers and put them into her own basket. Working together, they brought in a large quantity of the pale tubers, and she wondered how they would prepare them for cooking. After they washed their harvest thoroughly, Dove began slicing a big pile of them, which she intended to dry for winter use.

Before they were done with that task, the bigger boys came in with a pair of marmots, which they skinned out and gutted for cooking. "Now we cook the rest. You watch."

She dug a fire pit considerably deeper and wider than the animals, lined it with smooth river rocks, and built a fire in the cup. She kept the children bringing wood to keep the fire going, until the stones were crackling with heat, and when they were shimmering white, she scraped out the ashes with a long pole.

"Now you bring grass," she said to Katharine, who had wondered what use was going to be made of the big stack of green stuff the children had gathered. "Lay it in fire pit, very thick, while I wrap meat in leaves."

The meat went into the pit, surrounded by tubers, and they buried the entire pile beneath wet grass and leaves. Then Dove scraped hot soil from around the pit and covered the mound with that.

Everyone went about his or her work as usual, while the fire pit simmered along, but when Dove uncovered it late that evening the scent was wonderful. The woodchucks were so tender the meat fell from the bones, and the tubers were not bad, though Katharine found them slightly bitter.

She liked tule shoots much better, for they were crisp and juicy. The Shoshone seemed to understand that she was ignorant of such things, and as they proceeded on their journey they taught her what was edible, how to locate food plants, and how to harvest and cook them. It was the perfect season for that, for spring had brought everything up with a rush. Even plants that would bear fruit later in the year had leaves, so she could identify them when the time came.

It was a highly productive learning process. By the time the group reached the small valley where their trails parted, Katharine felt that she was fairly well equipped to deal with the rough country ahead.

With considerable sadness she watched the little band move away into the spring growth. Although she had been equally solitary while crossing the plains to the Bighorns, at that time she had been carried along by her own fury. Now that hot anger had died to ashes.

She was well away from her cousin, and whatever he did from now on was none of her concern. She couldn't be bothered even to hate him. There were more important matters to think of, mainly survival in this dangerous country.

She led Cuss along the game trail that skirted the stream her friends had told her to follow. "Keep water beside you, on left," Rabbit Catcher had said.

"When water go away between mountains, climb into forest and cross. Keep afternoon sun ahead until you see Ghost Mountains. Then you find another river to follow. Dry country past there. Good to have water close by."

She had heard old trappers back home speak of the Tetons, rising tall and pale against the sky beyond the valley of the Snake. Katharine wondered if she might not cut across at the end of that range, saving many weary weeks of travel.

Those who had trapped around Jackson's Hole mentioned trails leading around the southern end of the heights to the desert beyond. Surely there was a way, for the Shoshone admitted there was passable forest at the southern end of the Tetons, where the slopes gentled. If the old geezers she had listened to on trips to town with her father could cross there, surely she could, Katharine decided.

It was a long way, crossing steep ground that was covered, in places, with slides fallen from the adjacent heights. For days she struggled along, comforted only by the fact that there was plenty of grass for her animals and ample water for them all in the stream.

Sometimes she led Cuss and Sol down into the stream itself, as it grew smaller, shallower, and swifter. Aside from avoiding the slippages along the eastern side, this was a fine way of leaving behind no trail that even the best tracker might follow.

At last, however, as Rabbit Catcher had warned, the stream failed her, and she went ahead through forest that grew thicker, taller, and more intimidating. Above the treetops she could see another landmark she had been warned to watch for. Great gray peaks loomed above the trees, seeming to threaten to fall onto her as she passed.

Those were the upper heights of the Absarokas, the Crow Mountains, and she turned away from them with some relief, moving now through pines instead of firs and spruces. At times she emerged from a thicket on the side of a slope and saw the ghostly pale shapes of the tallest of the Tetons peeping through the trees.

She understood at once why her friends called them the Ghost Mountains. Like a row of waiting specters, they edged the sky as she descended, coming into view and disappearing again, sometimes for a day or more. They seemed to be draped in mists or clouds much of the time, which added to their ghostly appearance.

CHAPTER EIGHT

As she moved through the steep and forested country, Katharine found herself growing more and more lonely. It had been hard to leave the Shoshone behind, but unless she wanted to become an Indian herself, marrying one of the young men of the tribe, she had known she must.

She'd had no desire to marry at all, much less to become one of the hard-working wives who did all the necessary labor around the lodges. Just as well belong to Murray and be done with it, though she had to admit that she saw no sign of abuse of their families on the parts of the Shoshone husbands. They had seemed, to her surprise, to be fun-loving people, laughing uproariously at jokes she could not understand.

It had shocked her a bit that the children were seldom scolded and never spanked. Contrary to the beliefs of her own kind, the youngsters were alert, polite, and always busy. Their contributions to the family were as important as those of their elders, and everyone knew and appreciated that. This seemed to make them mature beyond their years.

She was thinking about that as she led Cuss up a steep trail that would take her over a series of ridges to the valley of the Snake. Dove had drawn her a map in the dust, not lines like a white man's map but carefully located dots that marked springs and wavering squiggles that were rivers and pointed shapes that were special peaks.

Beyond the Ghost Mountains was the desert she must cross, following the winding course of the Snake, which she could use as her guide to Oregon. Easy to think about, she decided, but hard to do. There were other tribes that hunted the country she must travel, and there were no guarantees of safe passage.

She tugged on the reins; behind Cuss, Sol grunted gruffly. He was loaded with *parflȩche* bags of pemmican and jerky, of deer hide for new moccasins, and of things she had brought from home. She had traded her iron pot and the extra pistol to the Indians for food supplies, thinking those a fair exchange for the valuable lessons they had taught her.

Pine squirrels chittered overhead, a hawk shrieked high above, and something grunted in the bushes ahead. Just what she needed, an old sow bear with half-grown cubs that would frighten her animals.

Katharine led Cuss out of the deer trail into a flattish stand of trees, and Sol followed, but his long ears were cocked, as if he were listening to something she couldn't hear. There was no way to go quietly with a horse and a mule in tow, but she went wide of the bear-noise, and soon was tangled in a copse of young fir trees.

She mounted Cuss, getting her head high enough to see over the lower growth, and found she could see a break up ahead. That helped, and before she had lost too much time she found herself on another trail, which also went the way she wanted to go.

Beyond the mountains, Dove had told her, the cousins of the Plains Shoshone were becoming impatient with the constant flow of white men into their country. "Take care," the woman had told her. "The painted skin that Catcher has made for you will tell their leader Washakie that you are a friend of our people, but young warriors are often impatient and do not think before they act. One dies as readily by the hand of a friend as an enemy."

Katharine didn't intend to test that theory. She would steer around any group of Indians whose trail crossed her own, if given the chance. Here she was still in the edge of the country of the Blackfeet, and those people never had liked white men; there was word that since the War began they had been even more warlike.

She disliked using a marked trail, even one that showed no track save those of deer, moose, and elk, along with those of smaller creatures. Yet the slope was so steep, often cut by ravines, and the growth on either side so thick that she had to use a game trail in order to proceed at all.

She made a dry camp on a long slope that was well timbered to hide her animals. She made no fire, chewing jerky for herself, and letting the horses nibble leaves and sparse patches of grass that found enough sunlight to sprout beneath the big trees, now that it was full summer. She hobbled both—there was no promise that the bear she had avoided earlier or another just as threatening might not spook the animals into the middle of next week.

She slept at last, but fitfully, waking at every night-noise. Before the black sky above the fir-tops turned gray, she was on her way again, after tightening the packs that she hadn't removed from the weary animals.

Remembering the cautionings of her friends, she stuffed a wad of jerky and the bone awl she had made while with the Indians into her bag of necessaries, which was always tied by a rawhide thong to her waist. You never knew what could happen here, the Shoshone told her, even when you were native to these chilly heights and experienced in all the dangers they held.

Then she led her animals up again, winding now around a considerable mountain, until they reached a broad shelf where some ancient slippage had torn away soil and trees and a great chunk of rock, whose side now formed a level place where she could rest and survey the countryside to the south. She could see for miles behind her, across ridges, peaks, and valleys, all cloaked in thick forest and ribboned with mist. The day was overcast, the breeze chilly, and she huddled her beaver-skin cloak, a gift from Rabbit Catcher, around her as she examined the way before her, the sheer drop beside her, and the cliff rising on her right.

She could hear nothing except the rush of wind through fir boughs, the trickle of gravel down the cliff above, and the heavy snorts of her animals. Yet she was not reassured. Something in her backbone told her there were enemies somewhere too near for comfort.

Primitive, inherited instincts made her hair prickle on her neck as she dismounted and tugged Cuss forward toward the shelter of the farther edge of the stony apron, where huge firs rose parallel to the cliff above them. Once out of the wind, she found she was still shivering. Not cold, then, but dread had her in its grip. Yet there had been nothing to see, nothing to hear that might threaten her.

She moved forward slowly, following a deer trail that skirted the mountain. Her ears were alert, even her nose sniffing for some scent that would warn of danger, but she could smell only the tang of fir and the winy air of the high country. She stopped to rest the animals some time past noon, finding a freshet spouting down a rocky runnel on the mountainside. She filled her water bags and let the animals drink their fill and graze on the sparse grasses beneath the trees. For herself, a bit of jerky from the big pack was enough to sustain her for a while longer, and before Sol and Cuss were ready she urged them on again.

Strangely, Katharine found herself wanting to talk to them, as if they were people. It must be that when a person was as alone as she, even the animals became companions. Yet she did not quite dare speak aloud, for that instinct still prickled in her neck and her back, making her wary as she moved along the narrow trail. In time that went over a low pass and emerged onto another mountainside, this one facing north.

The trail here was so narrow that she slowed even more, fearing that one of the animals might lose his footing. The drop below, though it was entirely cloaked in young fir near the top and much larger trees growing up from its depths, was obviously a long one. At eye level she could look into the tops of firs that were still of huge girth, even so far up. That meant their roots must be a long way down.

She was thinking about camping for the night when a shrill yell ahead made Cuss rear, jerking the lead rope from her hand. Another from behind made Sol try to bolt forward, which added to the confusion. Katharine, trying to find the rein again, felt the horse's chest bump into her so hard she flew into the air. Then she was falling, and she knew an instant of panic.

This time I'm a goner!

There was one instant when she bounced off something and tried to grab a handhold. Then she was off again, rolling, flailing, sometimes falling through tangles of growth, catching for an instant onto needled branches, only to fall again. Sometimes she rolled, bumping against trees, only to continue her downward course.

She didn't recall her final landing at all. When she opened her eyes at last, she knew she had either gone blind or night had fallen. She lay still for a moment, trying to decide if anything vital was broken, but as she checked arms, legs, neck, she realized that the thick growth causing the scratches and cuts that now burned fiercely on arms, hands, and face had also cushioned her fall enough to prevent serious injury.

She straightened her body cautiously, making no sound. Who knew if the attackers might still be searching for the owner of those richly burdened animals on the trail? Katharine listened now as if her life depended on it, which she felt it might well do. The flutter of an owl's call told her it was indeed night, and she opened her eyes again, trying to make out shapes in the darkness.

After a time, she found she could distinguish the thick bole of a tree that loomed over her, black against a paler shade that seemed to be the rock of the cliff behind it. She seemed to be well hidden from anyone above, which was probably what had saved her from being found.

She felt around her with both hands, trying to learn if she had good cover from anyone who came down the cliff to search for her, but she could find only thin stalks of weeds and broken branches of a bush. To her relief, her knife and hatchet and emergency pouch had not torn loose on her rough journey downward.

There had to be better hiding places, in case her enemies returned to search for her by daylight. She flinched as she rose to her knees, held onto the tree trunk and stood, feeling as if she had been beaten. Looking up through the fir branches, she could see a tiny patch of stars. There seemed to be nothing moving on the mountainside, when she stepped clear to see better, though she had no idea how far she had fallen.

Using every skill the Shoshone had taught her, Katharine moved toward the deeper darkness that seemed to offer concealment. Her seeking hands found a thick tangle, which she had to go around with great caution to avoid breaking twigs. Then she was in a sort of hollow, lined with ferns so thick they felt to her searching fingers like a miniature forest. Katharine slid between the stalks, working her way carefully into the middle of the mass. She hoped she left no sign at her point of entry, but she did not dare to turn and try to straighten any ferns that bent as she passed among them.

Then, exhausted and filled with fear, Katharine Salcomb laid her face on her arm and closed her eyes. She had done all she could do. Now her fate was in the hands of a God who had not treated her very well, so far.

* * * * * * *

She woke, feeling the vibration of a footstep on the ground beneath her arm.

Slitting her eyes, she found daylight had seeped down through the forest tangle and was lighting even the gray-littered floor of her hiding place. Her first instinct was to move, to ease her stiff limbs and test their strength, but her second was better. Lie still, it told her. Someone is searching for you. She waited, itches and aches and stings tormenting her, while the light grew stronger. When she could endure no more, she turned cautiously on her side and stretched arms and legs as well as possible in the cramped space she had made in the fern bed.

Now there was more vibration, as if something heavy walked nearby. A snuffling sound, a grunt, a squeal relieved her. It seemed to be a bear. And where a bear roamed, it was unlikely that any warrior might be looking for her.

She sat, very slowly, but even then her head did not rise free of the entangling ferns. Trying not to groan, she rose to her feet and stood motionless, for the bear was digging under a log only a few rods from her position. Beside the sow was a single cub, which was the source of the squeals each time he found a succulent grub.

With a sigh of relief, Katharine began backing slowly away, each toe seeking for secure footing behind her as she went. The bear raised her head and looked at her, the small eyes only mildly curious. Then she returned to her digging and her cub. Katharine left her to it, feeling more cheerful than she had believed possible.

She was grateful that the bag of necessities was still tied to her waist, scarred but undamaged by the fall down the cliff. She removed her beaverskin cloak, now tattered by trailing through the tangle, and cut a long thong from the fringe of her buckskin tunic, thanking her Shoshone friends once again for their gift. She replaced the frazzled thong of the pouch with a strong new one and sat on a rock to chew a bit of the jerky, wishing she had put more into that limited space.

Behind her was a bear, which she did not intend to disturb. Above, somewhere, were enemies—probably Blackfeet, given her present location. Down-slope she could hear the trickle of a stream, which she must visit to refill the canteen tied beside her necessaries pouch. Ahead, roughly, was the mountain range, where she intended to go, for behind that bear might come Murray, whom she intended to avoid even more carefully than that old sow.

The pattern she had learned in her journey so far was that streams followed the deep valleys between mountains. She would follow the one she heard until she found another way. Climbing that cliff was something she would not risk, given her present circumstances.

She blessed Dove and Rabbit Catcher for her extra moccasins. Riding boots would have left more distinct tracks and would have rubbed her feet raw. Now, on soft, moccasined feet, she made her way down to the brook, whose stony bed glinted with agate and jade and water-polished quartz.

Its water was cold and clean, and she drank deeply. The canteen was not as large as a water bag; she regretted the loss of those more than almost anything else. Ahead, over more mountains, past other enemies, lay the desert. There she would have to find some way to carry what she needed as she tackled its wide wastes afoot.

CHAPTER NINE

The time required to find the woman's route had taken entirely too long, and Murray was furious about that. Even then, the guide had done more guessing than tracking, and even now he was not certain of anything. They had lost a week in the effort, which One-Ear was careful to point out at frequent intervals as they searched and camped and searched again.

When Sun-Shot spotted the small group of Shoshone moving along the river he halted his mount and motioned for Murray to do the same. "There's some food gatherers over there. I'm going to talk to them, see if they've seen the woman. You stay here. They're pretty leery of white men, now, and it's only because I learned manners from the Cheyenne that I expect to get any answers."

One-Ear snorted and began pulling his rifle from its boot beside the saddle. "Just let me at the redskins. I'll make them talk," he growled.

"Like hell you will," O'Neill said. He turned his horse to block Murray's. "I'll do my job, but that doesn't include letting you mess with people along the way. I don't like you, Murray, and if I have to shoot you to keep you from killing innocent people, I'll do it. Else I'll cut your throat. And don't think you could move before I had you." He saw grudging agreement in the man's expression.

O'Neill could feel his face growing hotter by the minute, and by the expression in Murray's eyes he understood that his own must be blazing with anger. "I will go and ask, politely, if those women have seen Katharine Salcomb. You will stay right here." His hand clenched on the butt of his revolver, and Murray backed off, letting his rifle return to its place.

Sun-Shot dismounted and led Goldie some distance before he took off his side-gun and hooked the belt over the pommel of the saddle. He kept glancing back at Murray, half expecting the bastard to shoot him in the back.

When the shrill whoop told him a watching child had seen his approach, Sun-Shot held up his right hand, palm out, first two fingers extended and the others folded into his palm. Though too many white men had abused the sign of friendship in recent years, he hoped this group of gatherers was not in the mood for a fight.

A tall, thin woman came forward to meet him, her face impassive, her body tensed for anything that might come. She wore her hair in the Shoshone manner, and he spoke in that tongue.

"I greet you, Sister, on this bright day."

She relaxed minimally, though her face still showed no emotion. "I greet you, white man." She gave him no opening to introduce his question, so he disregarded good manners and asked it openly.

"I seek a woman, white like myself, who travels alone. That is a dangerous thing, and her...the man who is to look after her wants to bring her back home." The lie was bitter on his tongue, but he kept his face still and tried to conceal his distaste.

The woman allowed a crinkle at the corner of one eye to denote a smile. "We have seen no woman in danger," she said. "Our people seek food for the winter, and we have needs of our own. No white woman travels with us."

By then Sun-Shot could see that was true. Only another dark-skinned woman moved among the reeds along the river bank, several children helping her pick up something and put it into bags. Yet something about the phrasing of this one's answer made him wonder if her reply, while literally true now, might have been untrue in the past.

Though he could not push it, he felt almost certain these gatherers had indeed seen Katharine in their wanderings. Still, he would not have forced the facts from her if he could. He didn't really want to find his quarry, and that was the harsh truth. If these people had helped Katharine, they certainly felt the same or the woman would not have come so close to telling a lie.

"I thank you for your courtesy," he said. "I wish you well in your gathering, for it may be a hard winter." He pushed his hands forward, palms down, and lowered them in the sign of thanks.

The woman looked at him sharply, nodded once, and turned back to her duties.

She was someone he would like to know better, he thought, as he retraced his steps to Goldie and mounted to ride back to the waiting Murray. No nonsense about her.

Murray was sitting in the grass when Sun-Shot returned, his gaze fixed still on the small group of Shoshone. "Why'd you let 'em go?" he asked. "You could've killed the entire bunch before they could run. The more such vermin we get rid of, the better for us in the long run."

The guide felt a rush of anger again and quelled it with some difficulty. "You'd shoot a couple of women and some children, just to be doing something?" he asked. For two cents, he was thinking, he'd shoot Murray and get the one-eared fellow out of the clean world for good.

"They're redskins, aren't they?" Murray rose slowly and climbed onto his horse. "The day's going to come when everybody realizes that no white man will be safe out here until all the Injuns are dead and gone. You watch! Get this war over back East, and you're going to see a

slaughter of savages like nothing you could dream up."
His expression said that he'd enjoy every drop of blood
spilled.

That was too near O'Neill's own assessment, he found,
to argue. "That won't make it right or moral," he said,
jerking his head westward and setting off at a walk toward
the nearest route across the mountains.

"And you watch—one day somebody bigger and
meaner and better armed than we are is likely to come over
the horizon and wipe us out and take the land, in turn. Everybody'll be crying and wailing and wanting the govern-
ment to save 'em, and it won't be able to. Somehow that
seems fair, don't it?"

Murray's shocked look rewarded the thrust.

He ignored Murray then, keeping his eye on the
weather and the mountains, listening for any hint of a
threat sounding on the wind. He'd get this bastard to his
goal, if that was what it took, but when they found that
poor girl he wouldn't make any bets that he'd help his employer catch and subdue her. That wasn't the job he'd
signed on to do.

* * * * * * *

Katharine found the going a lot slower and more wearing as she trudged up and down ridges, slid down slopes to
save walking miles of angled game trails, and carried her
scanty bag of supplies. She figured the Indians would eat
the animals, and while Cuss deserved that and more, too,
poor old Sol had never been anything but a patient and
helpful beast. She hated to think of his life ending in such
a sorry way.

She missed talking to the mule while she traveled,
though soon she found she wouldn't have had the wind for
speech, even if he'd been at her side. Crouching in cold
camps, chewing carefully rationed bits of jerky, she kept

her ears tuned for any sound in the darkness.

Because of losing her supplies, she had to stop in the same spot for several days, setting snares for marmots or rabbits. Avoiding starvation wasn't her top priority, but it was just below keeping out of Murray's hands.

She had learned well, traveling with the Shoshone gatherers. Her snares produced a half dozen fat rabbits and two marmots, who had not expected to be trapped when popping out of their holes.

She skinned out the animals, rubbed their brains, along with ash from her tiny fire, into the raw sides of their hides, and dried strips of meat over the blaze. When she moved forward again she had patches for her moccasins, now wearing more quickly than before, and food that would last for some time. When she came at last down the long, wooded slopes out of the range behind her, seeing below the winding course of the Snake and the grassy flats that flanked it, she felt both relief and caution. There might well be trappers nearby, though summer was not the time when they trapped any of the rapidly diminishing beaver in the streams.

Katharine had known some of the old timers, back in town, and they did nothing to make her trust their likes if she should meet them in the wild. The tales they told had been both gory and obscene, and she had no desire to meet such men without help at hand.

According to Rabbit Catcher, the Snake ran south, here, around the end of the Tetons, before curving west and then northwest through the desert. She could see for herself that it was not large, as yet, lying flat and relatively narrow between grassy banks. If she could make her way across and keep to the toes of the snow-pale range beyond, she might manage to stay out of sight of anyone roaming the country.

It took days to reach the river, and she searched for a half day more to find a dead cottonwood that would float her to the other side. Once she drew that near the Ghost Mountains she began to feel the eerie sensation Rabbit Catcher and Dove had described to her.

"Spirits live there," Dove insisted. "They watch everything. You will see, if you go there. You will feel their eyes upon you. Be very careful, for those mountains drop snow or flood or rock upon those who go too near."

As she picked her way carefully among the boulders that had rolled into the valley between mountains and river, Katharine began to understand their concern.

Often she could see snowstorms raging above, hiding the tallest peaks in cloud and dropping occasional flakes even into the lowlands. Once she heard the rumble of a rock slide, somewhere among the heights. It sounded like wicked laughter, somehow, and she picked up her pace. She wanted to get clear of the Tetons as soon as possible.

She realized, all too soon, that following the river would take her too near the old trappers' refuge called Jackson's Hole. Indeed, as she drew near the last of the forbidding peaks, she climbed high on its lower slope, making for a height from which she could look out over the course she must take.

The Snake went very far to the south. If she cut across the lower elevations, she could go directly across its long loop and catch it as it swung northwestward again. There was no way, she had been assured, that you could go west without crossing the Snake again so she need not worry about losing her general direction.

At first the traveling was not terribly difficult. The slopes were steep, but by now she had toughened her muscles to conquer even the most demanding climbs. There was forest, and frequent streams ran down from higher elevations. But when, after days of effort, she crossed the final pass and saw before her the beginning of the desert she felt her heart grow heavy.

Katharine knew she must carry water if she was to

survive at all. This meant killing a deer, at least, and an elk if it was possible at all, using the stomach as a water bag. She had heard the great animals' belling as she traveled through the ranges. She had seen a number of them, back to the east. She knew the look of an elk track, now, and there were a few to be found here in this last bastion of forest country.

It took a couple of days to make two serviceable spears. She used her knife to tip one, fearing that it might be broken or lost, but not daring to risk anything less deadly for her elk trap. She found a trail, evidently used often as the big animals went down to drink in the stream that must run, at last, into the distant Snake. Alders and other small trees and bushes lined the way, and she found a spot at which the trail bent around a big fir.

As an elk turned to follow it, his neck would be at an angle. She would pull back the slender trunk and secure it with thongs from her buckskin tunic. A branch lying across the track would trigger the device—surely the spring of the green wood could whip the knife hard enough to stab deep into the animal's neck.

She set the trap carefully and hid every trace of her presence. Then she spent a day far from the spot, hoping her scent would drift away before nightfall. When the sun set, she was hidden in a thicket, watching and listening and hoping.

The first elk was a young one, which stepped over the trigger with blithe indifference and went on his way. The second was startled by a magpie shrieking suddenly overhead and bounded away through the bushes. The third was a mid-sized female, who stepped obediently onto the branch.

The whiz of the sapling, the thump of the knife occurred simultaneously with the cry of the elk. She shook her head, backed away, then fled down the track.

Katharine followed, her heart thudding with anxiety. If

nothing else, she must recover her knife. She found the elk some quarter-mile below, standing, now, her sides heaving, blood running in thick streams down her neck and foreleg. Katharine ran, her wood-tipped spear in hand. Using her momentum to add to her strength, she stabbed it deeply into the animal's side, at an angle, trying for the heart. The exhausted female dropped and lay groaning as she died.

Here was meat to dry for the journey, stomach and guts to clean and fill with water, bone to whittle into sharp edges in lieu of metal blades. Grinning, her face sticky with blood, Katharine began skinning out her prey with the knife, which was miraculously unbroken.

She was going to make it! If she lived and didn't break a leg, she was, by God, going to make it to Oregon!

CHAPTER TEN

Katharine had questioned the Shoshone closely about the country she must cross. They knew the country the French called the Tetons, and they also knew the desert west of that range. They had warned her that she must cross the wide water that ran along the foot of the range, before she could edge along to make the crossing on the southern end. At that point the Snake was relatively small, and she managed to swim its width without any problem. That was the easy part.

The mountains themselves were literally frightening. They stood like huge, snow-mantled ghosts above the narrow valley, and when she came to the southernmost of the big mountains she found little easing of the route. The declivities were steep and difficult to scale, and she often found herself sliding for long distances before she could catch herself and go on. It took days—she was too exhausted to count them.

Katharine came down out of the mountains at last, her second pair of moccasins already wearing thin. Her crude pack, whose supply of elk meat was dwindling fast, had worn calluses on her shoulders, but she trudged along doggedly. Behind her she had left everything she knew.

Now she had no horse, no mule, nothing but the vital edge against starvation.

Lacking even the old Hawken, she knew she would have to use every trick the Shoshone had taught her, if she were to survive a trek across the harsh country she now faced. Ahead stretched tan-gray lands, scabrous with gray sagebrush, that promised no water and little game that might fall to her snares. To survive, she knew she would probably have to eat lizards and insects and even snakes. The Shoshone had told her this was hard country, with few sources of water if you tried to travel due west. Yet they had said that the big river would cross your path again, for it wandered on a snake-crooked route, west and north and would intersect her course sooner or later, if she lived so long.

Dry, dun-colored mountains stretched along the north, and even drier desert country lay to south, east, and west. The tough gray sagebrush huddled close to its own roots, wasting no energy on tender shoots or leaves. Only an occasional scutter amid the brittle foliage told of the passing of some reptile or insect, all of which seemed to be colored so as to disappear against the arid earth. She would find some stream, she hoped, before she lost her battle to hunger and thirst.

The water she could carry in its elk-stomach bag was skimpy at best. The liquid was already stale, though she had filled it two days before at the last trickle she had found before descending into the desert. If she couldn't locate a stream, she would die, but somehow the idea was not as repugnant as it would have been a few weeks before. If One-Ear was behind her, as she felt certain he would be, then she would run until she dropped. He was welcome to her bones, if he could find them.

Katharine rationed her water tightly, using the Indian method of carrying a mouthful for a long distance, letting her tissues absorb it before swallowing the last bit. That kept her tongue wet and her salivary glands active, but it was very hard to keep from swallowing as she walked. She sometimes stumbled into holes or over hidden obstacles and swallowed inadvertently. Also she would hold in her mouth a smooth pebble she carried in her pocket, keeping her mouth moist. Her small supply of food was going entirely too quickly, as well.

When, on the fourth day, she came to a wide expanse of lava, lying in brittle ridges that seemed to go on forever, she knew she could go no farther in that direction. She wasted one day in scrambling among the crumbling terraces, which reduced her marmot-skin moccasins to ribbons. Her hands were sliced and sore, and knees and elbows suffered every time she fell.

When she backed out of the maze, she was almost spent. Dropping to sit on a bare patch between two clumps of sagebrush, she heard a tentative rattle deeper in the tangle. When she was much younger—a few weeks ago—she would have found the idea of catching a snake of any sort repugnant. Now her heart sped up and her body tensed.

She drew her knife out of its loop, moving so slowly that the reptile seemed not to notice, for its dry rustle continued. With her left hand she grasped a chunk of rock, which she flipped toward the sound.

There was a desperate flurry of rattling, but she was on her feet, heading toward the noise, which now stopped, replaced with the slither of the creature through the brittle leaves of the brush. She jumped a low clump of sagebrush, to see the reptile heading into a bowl-like depression. Then she was there, and the frantic snake was coiled in the bottom of its self-made trap, rattling frantically and making futile strikes upward toward the lip of the cup.

Katharine found another rock, this one very heavy, and dropped it onto her victim. It pinned the rattlesnake firmly enough to allow her to risk jumping into the hole. She lost no time in catching its tail, jerking it free, and smacking its head against the rock that had pinned it. Then she severed the head, climbed from the hole, and skinned the creature.

Raw rattlesnake was more delicious than she would ever have believed. Not only did it hold badly needed moisture, it was also tender and filling. She ate sparingly, spread the remaining meat on a bush-top to dry, and used the raw skin to mend her moccasins.

The meat gave her strength and allowed her to keep going, turning south toward the river that was still out of sight beyond the rolls of dry and inhospitable land. She was more than glad of the reinforcement to her footwear, for every part of this desert was rocky, thorny, and terrible on the feet. Even the tough snakeskin soon began to wear through as she fought clear of the last of the lava.

She had lost count of the days before she saw a patch of green at the very edge of the horizon. Cottonwood grew near water. That must surely mark the course of the Snake, looping its erratic way toward the northwest.

Two more rattlesnakes, a big rabbit, several lizards, and a small gopher saw her to the river. Already, so far up its course, the gorge was deep, the water swift, even though the runoff from winter snows had all but ceased with the arrival of midsummer.

Katharine made her way cautiously down the cliff to the water, where she found an apron of gravel on which to kneel as she drank. Only a handful did she risk at first, for she felt dried as old leather, and the Shoshone had warned her about drinking too much after long thirst. People sometimes died from that.

A huge cottonwood loomed over her, the shade feeling almost cool, after the sun-glare on the desert. A magpie swooped to light in the willows beyond the river, and she could see the gleam of his black and white feathers as he preened and posed. He looked fresh and cool and saucy, and she envied his ability to feed off the land so easily.

She sank onto her haunches and watched him. Where a bird was so unconcerned by the presence of man, surely small animals might easily be snared. Setting aside her pack, she looked intently at the edge of the river within her range of vision. There was a deep track worn into the rocky soil; probably antelope came down there to drink. Smaller runs marked the narrow strips of earth and gravel slanting down to the water, showing that other little creatures also watered there.

Katharine glanced up and down the cliff to either side of the cottonwood. It would never do to camp here, within reach of the river. Some distant cloudburst in the mountains could send a wall of water racing down to carry her off in her sleep. She needed a ledge well above the floodmarks.

Leaving her pack under the tree, she moved slowly along, keeping to outcrops of rock after she passed beyond the gravel strip, and rounded a slow bend in the stream. There the gorge widened and the water grew shallower, showing riffles of hidden rocks beneath the surface. On either side grew thick clumps of willows, and above the clump on her side lay a slanting ledge that led almost to the top of the cliff. There was even a sort of notch, where a chunk of stone had fallen away, forming a part of the ledge itself. She could camp there, rest, perhaps snare some meat. Then she would think what to do next. It was obviously impossible to walk across the country above her and come out alive.

Secure within the gorge, she could risk a fire, which she had not dared to kindle for a long while. She hoped the next day would find her with something she could cook over its coals. She knew she could snare small game, if any was there to catch.

There was plenty of deadfall drift caught behind the cottonwood and among the willows. Gathering a generous supply, she moved up and down the cliff, stacking it beside the notch where she would sleep. If all went well, she would rest here until she regained her strength and caught skins of some kind to make new moccasins.

Once she had her pack in place, her fire arranged, and the remnants of the last snake removed from her pack,

Katharine sank against the cliff, resting. When she woke it was almost dark, the water gleaming below her with the last pink glow from the sky.

She took from the thong at her belt her bag of necessary items, including flint and steel, along with a bit of tinder. She had made fire so often, now, that catching the spark amid the dry scrapings of moss and bark was almost easy.

Blowing it to a flame, she laid twigs over the small blaze, then thin branches, and at last larger bits of dead wood.

The dried strips of snake tasted much better when roasted, though she knew she would never relish it as the Shoshone did or as she had after a long fast. Still, with plenty of water at hand, she felt replete and content. Tomorrow would take care of itself. For tonight, warm and fed, she would sleep. If something killed her in the night, she didn't much care.

The pain in her cut, callused feet woke her. A jay was squawking in one of the willows, and a pair of magpies were flittering about, catching their breakfast, she supposed. The gorge still lay in purple shadow, but she could see high wisps of pink cirrus in the gap of sky visible from her camping place.

Today she would set her snares along some of the smaller runs down to the water. Perhaps she might catch something to eat, but if not she would wait with the patience she had seen among her Indian friends.

Hunger could be borne, particularly when there was no need for much physical exertion. Thirst was much harder to endure, but now, without that worry, she could relax, once she had the snares in place.

* * * * * * *

For several days she camped on the ledge. The first

night she caught a big rabbit and two smaller ones in snares along their run to the water. Those she skinned, ate much of the meat and put strips of the rest to dry.

The next night she caught a badger, which glared at her fiercely as she approached in the dim light of dawn. She knew from encounters beyond the mountains, as she helped to run the ranch, that this was a worthy opponent. Strong and mean and armed with sharp teeth and claws, the badger could defend itself against almost any enemy except one with a rifle. Getting in a hand-to-claw scrap with such a fighter was nothing she wanted to do. A serious injury at this point, with accompanying loss of blood, might mean her death; she was all too aware of that.

Backing away from the snarling animal, Katharine descended into the gorge again and went into the willow thicket. She found a dead branch that was fairly straight and still tough and strong. It was time to make another spear.

Sitting on a knee of stone, she split the end of the branch carefully and inserted her knife as far as it would go into the slot. Then she sliced fringe from her leather shirt and used it to bind the split tightly, securing the knife. It was an uncertain weapon, at best; it could be dangerous if it broke and left her within range of the badger's claws. A wounded badger would be far worse than one merely trapped. Its skin, however, would make a pair of moccasins that would be tough enough to withstand considerable wear. And who knew? Its meat might be edible, though the animal looked both old and tough.

She approached her prey from a different direction, working her way around to the farther side. Then, seeing the creature tense and hearing the increased volume of its snarls, she lunged forward and drove her spear into its back, pinning it to the ground. The great claws scrabbled at the stony soil, as a trickle of blood ran into the dust beneath the jerking body.

Katharine felt a bit ill as she leaned on the haft, sensing the death throes of her victim through the quivering wood. It was a handsome animal, even with its striped hide splotched with dust and blood. She hated killing things, and had always disliked shooting prairie chickens for the pot or slaughtering calves for beef. But now she understood as never before that if she was to live it meant that other creatures must die. Even the snakes had that right, and she had made a silent apology to the rattlers afterward, as she had seen her Indian friends do when hunting.

The badger gave a final jerk and went still. Katharine straightened her back and pulled her knife free of the body, wiping it clean by thrusting it into the ground several times. Then she caught the creature by a back leg and trudged away toward the river, trailing it behind her.

So large was the animal that its head dragged in the dust, leaving a bloody track. When she had deposited her game on the ledge, she wearily made her way upward again and used a brush-top to sweep dust over that trail. She wanted no predator following the blood to her camp.

It took all morning to dress out the meat, scrub the hide with ash and the creature's own brains, and stretch it to dry by pinning it to a flat rock beside her camp. After she had strips of badger meat (and it seemed to promise considerable toughness) hung up to dry, she took a long bath in the eddy beneath the cottonwood. She had enough to do for a while, and she needed now to rest and regain her strength.

Although she snared several more rabbits and a creature much like a weasel, she devoted most of the next couple of days to working the badger skin. Once it had dried in the sun, she scrubbed out the mix of ash and brain and laid the hide on a rock. Then, remembering Mourning Dove's technique, she scraped it clean and beat it with another rock, softening the stiff fibers.

By the time she was ready to leave her welcome refuge, she had a pair of badger-hide moccasins that wrapped about her ankles, protecting her lower legs.

She also had made rabbit-skin footgear, which she packed into a pouch made from more rabbit-skin. That would mean she could keep traveling, perhaps, without pausing too long in order to catch skins for making more.

Katharine knew it was time to go. If One-Ear Murray had decided to pursue her, he might have found a scout who knew his business. No matter how well she hid her trail, no matter how well the Shoshone might lie, if asked about her, a really good tracker would find traces.

It was time she headed west again, no matter how much she might long to remain here and live like an Indian or a hermit, fed by the land, her thirst quenched by the river. She knew now she could do that, but it might well mean being captured and returned to a life of slavery—and much worse.

CHAPTER ELEVEN

Sun-Shot O'Neill was disgusted. He had lost the notched mule track in the mountains, picked it up again for a time, though badly mixed with the tracks of other unshod animals, and then lost it, seemingly for good. He and Murray had searched the different routes up into the southern Absarokas without finding anything useful.

One-Ear was bitching again, and Sun-Shot had just about decided to find a good stout rattlesnake and put it into the bedroll with him before he had to shoot the man. He had been shutting his ears to the other's obscenities for hours, and when they stopped for the night he turned on his employer.

"Murray, we've lost the trail. We may not ever find it again, but that doesn't mean we can't find Katharine Salcomb. Her cousin told you their only kin left was an aunt in Oregon. That's where she's going, you can make book on it, so all we have to do is stop wasting our time looking for tracks that would be weathered out by now if we did luck onto her route.

"If we head west then north up the Yellowstone, cross the Bitterroots, and go on to the Columbia, it's more than likely we'll run into her or somebody who has seen her, when there's been time for her to get there."

Murray snorted, his eyes narrowing. "Got you beat, has she? A shirt-tail girl has beat the great Sun-Shot, friend of the Cheyenne. Why should I take your advice?

You've failed good and proper, and you owe me my money back."

Sun-Shot shook his head. "If you ever make it back to the bank you can take it and be damned. I'm not going back with you, however. I've taken a fancy to look around this country—never had the chance to take some time here for myself. Without me to guide you, you'll wind up over a cliff or snake-bit or scalped before you get back to the Bighorns."

He could see by Murray's expression that the man had already thought about it. He also knew there would be argument, because One-Ear Murray didn't know any other way to operate.

"I've got no intention of going around the long way. You think I didn't look at that map you drew? The Bitterroots will take us a long way north, over mighty rough country, before we get to the big river. Why not go right across here and then over the Tetons?" he asked.

"Look up there," Sun-Shot said, pointing at the heights that hung, black as paper cutouts, against the sunset. "Crossing the Absarokas takes more time than we've got. If you have to go this way, we'd better go south and up the Wind River, over the next heights, then down to the valley of the Snake. Once you see the Tetons, the last thing on earth you'll want to do is go skitin' up and down those bald peaks, with snow coming down even in midsummer or rockslides carryin' you down to grind you up."

Murray opened his mouth, but before he could speak, Sun-Shot went on, "West of the Tetons there's desert. Not just desert, you understand, but lava fields fit to cripple horse or man, dry ranges of hills, nasty country to travel through.

"If your...slave went that way she may well die there. If she didn't, she's probably going up through the Yellowstone country, like I suggested before, which isn't easy but is a damn sight easier than that route. With two good animals to swap off on, she can cover a lot of country fairly fast."

Murray snorted. Then he shrugged. "Maybe we'll find some sign of her on the way up the Wind River or somewhere this side of the Tetons," he said. "If we don't, then we'll go north. But I still don't like it."

O'Neill sighed. That had gone better than he expected. Maybe the country was getting to Murray—even he might be beginning to understand that this place cut you no slack.

"So in the morning we'll head south along the foothills, and by tomorrow night we might be cutting across to catch the river. It isn't bad going, as there's plenty of water at this time of year."

He turned on his side and closed his eyes, hearing from the wooded heights to the west the song of a wolf. That familiar sound sent him peacefully to sleep.

When he woke he was lying on his back, looking up into the dim face of a warrior in war-paint, who held a knife ready to slit his throat. Murray, barely within the angle of his vision, lay still and snoring, obviously sleeping hard.

As always, Sun-Shot had slept with his knife between his arm and his side. If he could kick aside his blanket quickly, he might have a chance with this adversary. Even as he had the thought, the man kicked the blanket away with his own moccasined foot and gestured for O'Neill to be very careful how he moved.

Damn! He sat slowly and cautiously, pushing the knife aside with his elbow, and the warrior kicked it away and out of reach. Beyond him, another shadowy figure slipped into view and bent over Murray.

Cut his throat! Sun-Shot urged silently, though he knew his parents would be dismayed at his un-Christian attitude.

However, the other Indian just pulled Murray up to sit,

groggy and bleary-eyed, staring at their captors. While he goggled, two more Indians arrived, silent and intent.

What's going on here? Sun-Shot wondered. If this band wanted horses, they could have taken them already. If they wanted weapons they were there for the taking. They certainly wouldn't want two grown men as slaves, for those were always more trouble than they were worth.

Dawn was creeping up as silently as the Indians had. As the light increased, he realized that these were Cheyenne, although he didn't recognized the war-paint designs of any of the four. However, at this point he would use any edge he could find.

"Greetings, my brothers," he said in Cheyenne. "I am the one called Sun-Shot by my second father, Stone Knife." He didn't elaborate on that, allowing the fellow with the knife to digest the words in his own good time.

After a moment, the painted face relaxed a bit and the hand with the knife gestured for him to stand. "You are the son of the Black Book People?" the warrior asked. "I have heard of you. There are those who say you are not our enemy."

"They are correct," Sun-Shot replied. "I am now scouting for that one...."—he nodded contemptuously toward Murray, who was staring, eyes round and white-rimmed, at the man standing guard over him. "We go to the Great River in the north."

The man laughed, the harsh grunt O'Neill was accustomed to hearing from his Cheyenne friends. "He seeks for a woman who has run away. We have heard the tale from a Shoshone captive. What kind of man is he that his woman must run from him?"

"A cruel man, who is not her husband and has no real right to her," O'Neill said. "I scout only because I must care for my old parents, who are sick.

"Are we your captives? Or will you let us go forward on our own business?"

That was a bit forthright, he knew, for Indian tastes, but he had no desire to remain in doubt about their status.

Murray turned his head and glowered at them both. "What's the savage saying?" he asked. "They going to kill us?"

A thump on the head silenced him, and Sun-Shot nodded with satisfaction. It was time One-Ear got some of the treatment he so liked to give others.

He hadn't expected to get off scot-free. You didn't when trading for your life with Cheyenne. But a pack horse, two extra blankets, and gunpowder seemed a small price to pay for keeping his scalp, and even Murray raised no objections.

Until later, it turned out. Once the Cheyenne had left them to pack up what was left of their goods and supplies, he began to grumble, then to curse. Before Sun-Shot had Goldie saddled, ready to go, he was almost ready to call back the Cheyenne and turn One-Ear over to them.

He rode well ahead of Murray, turning to the south to skirt the foothills, heading toward the rough country that lay between the Absarokas and the Tetons. It took two long days to come to the Wind River, at a point where it had already begun to lie far down between the ridges that flanked it.

The country was lush now, for summer had greened the slopes, making good grazing for the horses. They were now in high country, which meant the days were not extremely hot, and they made good time, following the stream on a track that lay along the slope above it.

With Murray grumbling along behind him, Sun-Shot moved cautiously, for this was the time of year when hunters were abroad, and war parties made their way toward the herds of enemy tribes. He found traces, too, of unshod ponies, although among the tracks he could find no hint of the nicked hoof mark he was hunting.

They camped high, each night, when he could find a

way to climb the steeps.

They had left the river behind, veering into forests of fir and alder, where the nights were cold and snow still hid in the shadows of huge tree trunks. Sun-Shot scouted the area, every evening, before they camped, and they built no fire, though Murray grouched about that, too.

"You remember the Cheyenne? Well, remember something else. I have no friends among the Shoshone or the Paiute or the Blackfeet. If we waked up with any of them standing over us, we'd die. So shut your mouth and keep up." He tried to sound even meaner than he felt, which was hard to do.

They had camped early, one evening, because he remembered the lay of the land. Tomorrow, he felt, they would cross over onto the downslope leading at last to the valley of the Snake that lay at the feet of the Tetons.

He felt obscurely uneasy, and at last he moved along the ledge on which they had stopped, moving back eastward where the shelf of rock narrowed. Even in the twilight, he could see that something had fallen off the cliff on the other side of the ridge, for branches had snapped and were now withered brown. A scrape on the rock at the edge spoke of a desperate hoof, as well.

Could this be a sign that the quarry had come this way and had fallen into the deep glen below? He moved farther east, but there was no other sign. Then he went west, passing a drowsing Murray, to follow the ledge around a belly of stone and onto a wider spot.

A fire had burned there, some time ago. Around the blackened spot were fragments of bone. He searched among the gnawed bits, finding the leg-bone of a horse— or a mule? The bone seemed very thick and heavy for a horse's leg.

And then he found, discarded, that notched hoof he had followed for so long.

He took it up and set it in a patch of dust. That was the

mark, he knew.

There was no sign of a woman, but he knew too well the needs of the Indians here. Nothing would be wasted, no cloth or metal, no boot or hat or weapon. They would have taken everything, probably including the woman.

Still, he remembered that broken branch and the mark on the ledge. Had she managed to escape even from this fate? He might know, if he could search down the almost sheer declivity beyond the hoof mark.

He went back to camp and crouched to unroll his blanket. Murray groaned and sat to cough and spit. "Find any sign?" the man asked gruffly.

Sun-Shot looked up at the dark shape that almost merged with the approaching night. "Yes, I did," he said.

Murray lunged to his feet. "Well? You tell me, right now, or I'll shoot off your ears."

"Do that," Sun-Shot growled, "and I'll leave you right here to root, hog, or die. Tomorrow I'll show you what I found. The sign is old—maybe weeks old. Another night won't make a bit of difference. Now go to sleep, you one-eared varmint, before I bite off your other ear."

Nevertheless, O'Neill woke early the next morning, before the sky had paled enough to let him see. He grubbed out a bit of jerky from his pack and drank from his canteen. As the sky grew lighter, Murray stirred and rose to stagger off to the edge of the rock, to pee into the fir-darkened space beyond.

When he returned, he ate a bit and then turned to Sun-Shot. "Now then. You going to show me or not?"

O'Neill nodded. "This way. You won't need your horse—it's only a hundred yards or so. Stay right behind me, because the ledge narrows as it goes."

Again he followed the rocky way and again he spotted that withered branch some thirty feet down the abrupt cliff. "See that?" He pointed.

Murray squinted. "What's so special about a broken

limb?"

"Where it is." Sun-Shot knew he sounded impatient, but it seemed very clear to him and it should have been to Murray, as well.

"What could break that branch? Nothing standing on the ground, because it's halfway up a mighty tall tree. Nothing reaching out from the ledge, because it's at least twelve feet from the nearest point. Something fell, pitched off, most likely, and hit that branch coming down."

Murray gave a grunt. "You think it was her? She fell off down there? What about her horses."

"The reason she fell might have been because her horse was startled by Indians. I found horse—or mule, is more likely—bones west of our camp. That war party had itself a feast, and I'd bet it was on Miz Salcomb's animals."

"You don't think they got her, then?"

"If they did, then who fell off this cliff? Indians are as sure-footed as it gets. No horse went off down there or there'd be a lot more branches broken on the way down. Something fairly small and light got shot off down there. If I go down, I might be able to find some trace of what it was."

Murray sat on a knee of rock and stared for a moment into space. Then he sighed, put his elbows on his knees, and said, "Then you go on down and see. I won't risk myself on such a hare-brained scheme, but if she's dead, there's no reason to spend more money chasing her."

Sun-Shot shook his head. "If you don't care any more than that about her, why'd you want to marry her?"

"Marry her? Hell, man, that's why I bought her. No courting, no marrying, but I'd have a woman when I wanted her, along with somebody to do the work and cooking. It would be fun to break her to the saddle, but other than that I don't give a damn. Sending good money after bad's not the Murray way."

LONE RUNNER, BY ARDATH MAYHAR

As Sun-Shot started down, holding tightly to the rocky cliff with both hands and bracing his feet against handy tree trunks, he found himself feeling extremely angry. What a nasty fate for a young woman who, far as he had ever heard, never did anything worse than training colts and taking care of her daddy!

CHAPTER TWELVE

Katharine began her long trek along the edge of the river canyon, watching the strong current below carry debris from the now-distant mountains to the east. The walking was hard, and often she found herself sprawling after an unguarded step. When she came to a sharp bend that had caught a great deal of debris that included some good-sized trees, she knew the time had come to build a raft. That would allow the river to do the work for her, as she had hoped she could do.

The current was dangerous, she could see. Drowned animals sometimes bobbed on the current or hung in drifts of sodden fur on snags or in eddies, and she had no desire to join them. No, she must be careful and she must be clever, if she was to find her aunt in Oregon before anyone from the east could catch up with her. A raft was the most effective way she could think of to gain distance, if Murray should be behind her.

She at last found, caught in one of the many bends of the river, a drift that offered good-sized logs and more branches and snags than she could ever want. The drop from the cliff-top to the water-side was steep, but the walls of the canyon were gullied and uneven. She managed to climb down at last to reach the narrow strip of rocky beach along the stream. Out of breath, she rinsed her bruised hands in the edge of the water and inspected her prospective raft materials.

Cottonwoods and willows, broken-off branches, and washed-out stumps from miles upstream had grounded on upthrust stones and were piled like jackstraws in the rocky curve of the canyon. More than one winter's snowmelt had supplied elements of that drift, and some of the logs below the water level were soft, almost rotted away.

The upper level, woven together by current and pressure, seemed to be more recent arrivals, still solid enough to suit her purpose. The tangle, anchored against a pile of boulders fallen from the cliff above, blocked the northern side of the river so that it roared and muttered around the obstacle as it rushed past.

She drew a deep breath, realizing the magnitude of the task before her. While she rested and thought, she searched the crannies in the canyon wall for food. A couple of lizards fell to well cast rocks, and she located runs where small creatures came down to drink. She had found such tiny trails convenient for her traps, as she journeyed, and she set snares before beginning to work at loosening the foundation for her raft.

Although the noise of the river drowned out any sound of approaching danger, she felt safer concealed in the canyon's depths than she did on the edge of the desert above, where any upright figure could stand out amazingly clearly. If she did not detect anyone moving toward her because of the noise of the water, no one approaching would have any indication that she was there, either. As long as there was no cloudburst far upstream along the Tetons or in the mountains this side of that range, she could remain here fairly safely for as long as it took to build her transport.

Clambering around the upper edge of the drift, she surveyed the downstream side. It made more sense to construct her craft there, where she would not have to find a way to get past the obstruction. An eddy behind the drift offered a place to assemble her materials, for she waded in and pulled a floating log far enough ashore to anchor it across the opening that would allow her materials to escape into the downstream current.

By the time she had prepared her work area, the sun was down behind the canyon wall. Wet and cold, she decided to build a fire. With all that wood, it would be foolish to risk sickness when she might as easily get warm and dry again. Down there in the canyon, with bends both upstream and down, there seemed little chance that the light could be seen beyond her niche between the stone wall and the tall pile of driftwood.

Her rabbit skin pack now held strips of dried meat from many kinds of animals and reptiles. Carrying with her a store of food was, she found, the only way to be sure she would eat enough to retain her strength.

She roasted stringy lengths of rattlesnake over her bed of coals, once the fire had dried her moccasins and warmed her through. The hot meat, even lacking in fat as it was, felt solid in her belly, and she was soon drowsy.

Now that summer was waning into autumn, the nights were cold. Her beaver cloak had long since been shredded to rags and she had used the scraps to mend her moccasins. She was glad that she had patched together a blanket made of different kinds of furs and hides. It lacked a lot of being as warm and comfortable as her mother's woven bedcover, but it was far better than lying on bare stone with nothing over her but stars. As soon as she had covered the coals with dust and checked her snares, she rolled up in her odd blanket and went instantly to sleep, despite the pebbles and shards of stone that poked through her scanty bedding.

The sound of squeaks and struggles in the night brought her up again to find the moon peering down between the towering walls. That offered enough light to allow her to check her first set of snares, and there she found a couple of skinny rabbits kicking and squealing. She broke their necks neatly and went to find her other quarry.

The loop she had hooked to a young willow held a snarling creature something like a ferret, which seemed so fierce that she backed away in order to plan her mode of handling it. Getting scratched and bitten would risk infection, and she couldn't afford to get sick, so far from any source of help.

At last she slid back down to the tangle and located a long branch, still solid enough to make a good tool. She regretfully sliced off another of the useful thongs that fringed her Indian shirt and formed a slip-knot at the end of the stick. The trailing end was some twelve inches long, leaving enough to allow her to pull the noose tight around the creature's neck.

It took some positioning to get the loop in place, for the animal seemed to guess her purpose and kept twisting in the snare. At last she dropped the noose over its head and pulled the thong hard.

The feel of the little beast's struggles at the end of her stick sickened her, but she kept on until it was dead. Even if its meat proved to be inedible, she needed all the animals she could get, for they formed her source of moccasin patches, twisted-fur cord, and sinew.

She secured the carcasses high in a willow tree and returned to her blanket.

Tomorrow she would need to be rested, in order to begin her wrestling match with that pile of dead wood.

* * * * * * *

She rose as soon as she could see and chewed some cold rattlesnake meat for breakfast. A brisk wash-up in the edge of the eddy made her skin tingle and her blood race, for no matter what the season, the river seemed to be pretty chilly.

She decided to skin off her clothing, to keep from getting soaked. In that super-dry air, water dried instantly on the skin, but clothing took a bit longer. Though she felt a bit odd at first at being naked in broad daylight, she soon found herself busy enough to forget her misgivings.

She worked at the edges of the drift, loosing smaller bits to free up larger ones. At last she freed a good-sized piece of tree trunk, cottonwood, she thought, and floated it out of her way. That seemed to unblock another batch of stuff, and before the sun was overhead she had a considerable flotilla of logs bobbing gently in her pool behind the barrier.

In two days she had enough to make a raft that promised to be broad enough for stability. She moved the logs around in the pool until she had them in some kind of workable order, the longest in the middle, tapering off with shorter ones on either side. Then she looked around for something with which to bind them together. She had found willows growing wherever there was water, and along the Snake it was no different. Long, flexible willow boughs promised to work, if she managed to weave them together securely around her poles. She worked swiftly, now; this late in the summer she needed to, because winter would come, before very long, to the mountains which she must cross.

She hoped she would find some inhabited place to live and work, if necessary, if she could not make it to Oregon in time. At least she might work to earn better blankets and a good axe and perhaps even a rifle. It was much easier to shoot game than to snare it, and large animals gave her more energy than small ones did.

She did not pause while considering, however. Instead, she sliced off long willow withes with the knife that had traveled in her boot or tied to her body, all the way from Wyoming. When she had a pile gathered, she carried armfuls to the edge of her pool and arranged them conveniently. Weaving the long strands over and under the logs, she back-wove or tied the loose ends with more strands from her leather shirt. In two days she had a raft that was part log, part wicker-work.

She searched for a long time before finding a pole long enough to use as a sweep for guiding her awkward craft, and that she set into a gap deliberately left for the purpose, securing it with a forked branch that seemed very hard and strong. She tried the thing experimentally before setting off down the current, and her main worry was that her lack of body-weight might make it impossible for her to manage the sweep in rough water.

She had caught game in her snares while she worked, skinning them and drying the furs. When she was ready to leave she had quite a bit of dried, smoked meat and a bundle of furs to add to her blanket or with which to repair clothing or moccasins. After losing everything in the mountains, she realized that it would be even easier to do that afloat.

That was why she fixed willow hoops to the middle of the raft, looped fore and aft, to which she could bind her supplies tightly. Even if the raft came apart in rapids or was dashed against the stony walls of the canyon, she might retain some part of her food and furs, she hoped.

On the fourth morning of her stay beside the drift, she pushed her barrier free of the shore and allowed her raft to nudge its way out of the pool. The sun was still well down behind the rock wall, and the air was chill. The canyon smelled of wet stone, tanged with sage and something that smelled sharp in the nostrils.

As she set her feet and held the sweep tightly before moving out into the current, Katharine felt a surge of excitement. She had been running away, until now. But with her departure, this time, she felt that she might be running toward something. Toward, perhaps, a life that could be both useful and happy?

That might be a lot to ask, in this hard world through which she traveled, but at least she could find a way to make her living. Surely there would be a need for her skills, if not at training horses, then at working about a ranch or a farm, or even (she frowned at the thought) at housework.

The current caught the rough bow of the raft and pushed it downstream. She had tucked her feet into the willow weave, and now she held tightly to the sweep, finding it as contrary as a young horse. Still, she clung to it as the raft bucketed down the river, often driving far too near for comfort to jutting boulders or unexpected islands rising from the river.

This was a quick way to cross the country, she realized, as she did her best to guide her contrary craft. The danger only added to her exultation, for amid the chaos of current and stone and rapids and rocks, she knew that even the best tracker could hardly find her now.

She had left the lava country long before, and that held no tracks. She had taken care to leave no sign on the desert above the river, and when she broke camp beside the drift, she had worked hard to restore both the tangle and the surrounding area to a natural-looking state.

Water could not betray her path, and One-Ear Murray, if he followed at all, would never find her now.

CHAPTER THIRTEEN

One-Ear had been reluctant to allow his guide to take off down the abrupt drop on the off-chance that his quarry had fallen there, but Sun-Shot used all his powers of persuasion. The clincher, he thought, had been his argument that if Katharine was lying at the bottom of the glen, dead as a doorknob, Murray would be wasting his time and money if he went any farther.

However, as O'Neill cinched a rope around the nearest tree that offered support and began moving down the slope, steadied by his line, he found himself convinced that he would not find her there. She had done too well, had moved too surely across this harsh country to die by accident, he felt.

Others had died so, many times, but this was someone cut from different cloth. He had no intuition that she was anywhere but up ahead someplace, still doggedly struggling forward. Afoot. The thought came to him suddenly as he clambered around a leaning spruce to continue his descent. The remains of her animals were up there on the trail, he knew, for that notched hoof was as familiar to him by now as his own footprint.

That added another dimension to her problems, but as he mulled it over, while deftly avoiding obstacles in his way, he had the unshakable feeling that she would not stop, if she had to crawl. He found himself mentally urging her on. No one with that sort of grit deserved to have anything to do with the likes of One-Ear Murray.

He reached the bottom of the cliff some six hundred feet below the end of his rope. There was, of course, no sign that anyone had fallen there. It had been too long since the bushes had been disturbed, and the rampant growth would have covered any trace. However, he ranged widely along the bottom of the glen, checking the narrow stream and the area on either side.

He found sign of a she-bear and her cubs, her wide paw-prints imprinted in soft ground amid ferns. This was obviously their normal range, for fresh ones overlaid the older marks.

He grubbed about, still searching, and in a thick tangle he found the torn-off end of a leather thong. It was from the sort of deer hide shirt worn by warriors, and yet he felt sure it had been on the back of Katharine Salcomb.

She might have traveled for a bit with the Shoshone he had questioned, for he had felt they were not telling him what he wanted to know. It was quite possible she had traded with them for that useful garment. He'd worn one for years, and there had been times when he'd returned after months of tracking or scout work with most of his fringe gone, used for vital needs along the way or lost in just such tangles as this one.

Feeling more cheerful, he returned to the spot where he had come down and began to climb. There were many trees rooted into the slope, and it was less trouble to climb to the level of his rope than it had been to come down without going too fast and bashing out his brains.

When he peered over the top, at last, he found Murray dozing against the rocky outcrop beyond the path. "Not there," Sun-Shot said, as he pulled himself onto the ledge. "So we can go on, knowing at least that she isn't lying dead down there. I found a scrap of thong that may have come from her shirt."

Murray opened an eye and stared at him. "You sure?

No bones or anything? Wild animals can destroy bodies, you know. If she's dead I certainly don't want to spend any more looking for her."

Sun-Shot shook the dust and needles from his clothing and began rolling up his line. "I know the signs when a body's been messed around by varmints," he said. "Except for some bear tracks and signs of marmots and such, there's nothing down there that could be human traces, except for this bit of leather."

He tied the line to his saddle and tightened the girth. "You ready to ride? If she fell down there, she didn't climb up here again, that's for sure. For one thing, there had to have been Injuns on this trail, or her horse and mule wouldn't have been eaten up there ahead.

"Probably one of 'em smelled the warriors and shied and bucked her off down the mountainside. I hope she had a pouch of necessaries tied to her, or she was left without anything at all, weapons, food, or fire-makin's."

Obviously Murray was uninterested. He didn't even grunt as he tightened his girth and mounted his horse.

Sighing, Sun-Shot heeled Goldie in the ribs and moved back up the ledge toward the scene of the feast of horse-flesh. The ledge widened after that point, gradually turning into an apron of rock that curved with the mountainside and led at last to a downward slope.

As he rode around a knot of fir trees, O'Neill saw the ghostly peaks of the Tetons, rising in the distance. As usual, they were pale with snow. A shawl of cloud was wrapped around the head of the tallest, promising more.

"She either went up toward Yellowstone or she went south of the Tetons," he called over his shoulder. "Better be makin' up your mind, because sooner than later we've got to go one way or the other. Quickest would be by way of Yellowstone, for we could wait for her near settled country."

Murray spat against an unoffending rock and

shrugged. "I think she'll go the direct way," he said. "She's got no mount, any more. Maybe she'll wear out along the way and we can pick her up without a fight."

Sun-Shot rode onward, remembering the terrible country beyond the mountains.

Desert, lava beds, dry country that could kill even an Indian, if he had bad luck.

* * * * * * *

They rode into Jackson's Hole three days later, their horses weary and their own bones aching. In this high country, even summer didn't mean you wouldn't have to ride through a snowstorm.

The Rendezvous that had been held there a decade before had left no trace, though there was a huddle of shanties in the cup sheltered by the abrupt wooded heights that loomed over it. Even though the beaver were growing scarce, it was clear that some persistent fur-hunters returned here in winter to set their traps. This was not trapping season, however, and they saw nobody for some time. At last they came into a flatter area where a big log structure emitted a plume of wood smoke. Sun-Shot dismounted and called, "In the house! Anybody there?" This would tell anyone present that his intentions were friendly and he posed no threat.

A heavy step sounded inside, and in a moment a giant of a man stepped onto the creaking boards that formed a sort of porch. "Now who might ye be, Stranger?" the fur-clad behemoth asked. "An' why be ye here in summer, when even if there wuz beaver they'd be in no shape for the fur trade?"

"We're not trappers," Sun-Shot replied, before Murray could open his mouth. "This fellow is searching for his woman, who might've come this way a few weeks back. You seen a small kind of woman with reddish brown hair?

Name of Katharine."

The man-mountain burst into a guffaw that all but shook the towering heights around them. "A woman? Man, if there'd been a woman in a day's ride in any direction, I'd've smelled her out an' caught her for myself. Haven't seen a white woman in three year, and believe you me, that whets up your senses a whole damn lot. No, you're either crazy with the sun or she went another way."

He cocked his head and stared down at them quizzically. "Travelin' alone, was she? Man, if that was the case, she's long dead and gone from this worl'. No white woman would last till the water got hot, out here in the high lonely. If critters didn't git her, Injuns would. Or mountain men, who kin get a bit wild, their ownselves."

Sun-Shot nodded. "Ordinarily, I'd agree," he said. "But this is one slick, quick, smart lady. I suspect that if she came this way she might've gone wide of here, maybe edgin' up into the mountains till she got clear of any sign of people. We might's well go on a bit to see if we can pick up sign, anyway."

He dismounted and turned again to the big man. "We need some things, if we're to cross the desert off to the west. You got any extra water skins? We could use some, if you do. Horses drink a lot, and men get dried to the bone in that country over there. The way I recall it, that's a nasty journey."

"Come inside," the fellow said. "My name's John Bodger, and I ain't had company for weeks, now. I think I got some skins in the back. Come in and be welcome. Got a deer haunch on the fire right now, iffen you're hungry."

Once Sun-Shot introduced himself and Murray and got the polite preliminaries out of the way; he found Bodger affable enough, though there was nothing at all civilized about him. In fact, he smelled like a wolverine, and Sun-Shot wondered if he ever washed himself. A second whiff persuaded him that he didn't.

The giant had a fire roaring in a rock fireplace into which he had fitted six-foot logs. Evidently, Bodger liked his comfort, though the warmth made his personal fragrance almost unbearable.

The meat over his fire was, however, doing its best to overcome that. As juices dripped onto the coals and sizzled, Sun-Shot found his belly growling. Murray, who lacked all the manners O'Neill had learned at his mother's knee, was already hacking off a chunk with his boot knife, and Bodger didn't seem to mind.

With a silent apology to his mother, who had strained a gut to teach him mannerly ways, Sun-Shot drew his own knife from his boot and began whittling off strips of meat for himself. In an iron pot edged into the coals, something simmered, but Sun-Shot couldn't tell from the smell if it might be some sort of wild root or Bodger's socks. He didn't attempt to try it, and even Murray avoided the steam wafting up from the bubbling mess.

Once his belly was full of hot venison, O'Neill began exchanging news with Bodger. "You mean Lincoln done freed all the slaves?" the big man asked. His tone held more than a bit of incredulity. "Nex' thing you know, they'll be givin' women the vote! The worl's gettin' to be a strange place, Friend, and I don't much keer to go back and jine up with it."

Sun-Shot hid his smile. He'd known a lot of people who felt the Emancipation Proclamation flew in the face of God and nature, though his own family had always preached against slavery. "That's what they tell me, anyway," he said. "The war's taking a long time, and it seems people back East are trying every way they can think of to shorten it up. I hear that England may stop supplying the South, because of this, and that could mean the end for the Confederacy." He sighed, thinking that people were always doing good things for bad reasons.

Bodger nodded. "Now that's somethin' I kin understand," he said. "You git somethin' you need for it, it makes more sense. Then after things settle down agin', they'll prob'ly ketch all them black folks and put 'em back to work."

As that was one thing his parents had feared all along, Sun-Shot didn't find Bodger's instant thought of it comforting at all. However, he said nothing more about that, listening, instead, to the mountain man's account of the winter's trapping and the prospects for the fall.

"It ain't good, an' that's a fact," the man said. "The beaver's gettin' all trapped out up in the Swans and the Bitterroots. Back east of the Divide, the business is just about dead, worse than it is here. Too many beaver's been took out of the mountains, and that's no lie. We kind of thought, back in the Forties, that there was no end to 'em, but we was wrong."

He leaned back in the heavy chair he'd built from birch poles and upholstered with furs. The firelight danced on his weather-lined face and kindled red glints in the white hairs of his beard, as he stared into the flames.

"We just plain put ourselves out of business," he said softly, and Sun-Shot felt certain those were words he often said to himself here in his lonely shanty.

* * * * * * *

The next morning, O'Neill and Murray set off toward the southwest, intending to climb the less forbidding slopes south of the main Teton Range. Bodger assured them that horses could manage it, though there were places where they would be forced to walk and lead the animals past dangerous areas.

They covered the distance to the slopes in a half day. By mid-afternoon Sun-Shot was stopping to rest his mount often, for the slope was steep and the animals, even the pack horse carrying the water and other supplies, tired quickly. Behind him, Murray was, as usual, grumbling. "It will take us forever to get across at this rate," he growled. "If I'd wanted to get an old hag, I could've found a bunch of them back where we came from."

"If you want to be on foot, like she must be, you're welcome to ride ahead as fast as you want until your horse drops dead under you," Sun-Shot said, over his shoulder. "I think you'd find climbing this might be easier by yourself, but when you came to the desert beyond you'd change your mind in a hurry." He caught his temper and hauled it back under control.

"Now you just come along and think about the desert yonder, and the lava beds, and the long, long miles of nothing that you'd have to foot it across, and be thankful for what you've got." O'Neill spat off to the side and moved ahead.

If he ever got through with this job, he'd take a lot closer look at any future employer, that was for damn sure.

CHAPTER FOURTEEN

Katharine had not imagined that rafting down the river might be so terrifying. Though the river seemed calm, the current was swift with the runoff of snows that midsummer heat was melting in the Tetons and the lesser ranges flanking them.

The high cliffs shot past at dizzying speed, as she tugged at her steering oar and struggled to keep her makeshift craft from crashing into them in places where the river curved sharply. Occasional tumbles of rock in midstream required her utmost strength, as well, and she realized that she had quite possibly bitten off more than she was physically able to chew.

As gouts of water rolled over her feet and splashed into her face, she held on to the oar with grim determination. A clean death by drowning was better than anything she might expect from One-Ear Murray, if he followed her. She had seen her father and mother out of life, and now there was no real need for her, anyway.

The scent of water on stone was sharp in the corridor the river had cut into the rock of the plain. Occasional clumps of willow or cottonwood marked the descent of tributaries into the main stream, and the lines of green came and went so quickly she had no time to turn the clumsy craft into a quieter channel to rest. Feeling each time as if she were about to die, she found herself avoiding catastrophes that should have swamped her. Practice gave her more skill at managing the sweep, as well, and before the sun had disappeared behind the cliffs she spotted a wide channel ahead, where a patch of green told her she might find refuge at the mouth of a tributary.

As she had learned on her headlong dash downriver, the secret lay in preparation, so by the time she came to the slow bend holding the mouth of the smaller stream she had already begun swinging the clumsy nose of the raft toward the right. As soon as she made it free of the main current, she found it easier to guide the raft into calmer waters, where only a trickle now descended from the rock into the river. Beyond that the wall of the canyon swung out to form a loop in the river, and in the shelter of that cove she grounded her raft at last.

Shaking with stress and exhaustion, she secured it to a big cottonwood whose bole was huge and gray and shaggy, witness to long years of survival here where water was the secret of life. Its roots must run deep, she thought as she dropped onto the gritty stone beside her raft and closed her eyes.

Katharine had intended to rest only for a moment, but when she opened her eyes the sky was dark and stars blazed above. Their reflections gave a tenuous light there in the cove, and she sat up, only to find her body almost beyond moving. Every muscle, every bone, even her teeth seemed to hurt with a separate pain.

Only her long years of controlling horses, of working with her father at building fences and hauling supplies and carrying hay had given her strength to survive this first day of travel on the river. Now she wondered if she could last out the journey down the Snake. Would the merciless river give her time to toughen to the task, or would some unexpected rapid or sharp bend or midstream boulder put an end to her reckless venture?

As she began to move, she knew that death would be far preferable to day after day of such misery in her bones.

Before she set out again she had to rest, to eat well, and to secure her hard-won supplies to portions of the raft that were large enough to survive a run through impassable rapids. Since her time with the Shoshone, she had kept basic needs like flint and steel, her knife, and such vital necessities in a pouch tied securely to her person, but those would not be enough supplies to see her to her aunt in Oregon, if she should lose the rest again. Here there was no rich mountain forest to use in rebuilding her tools for survival.

She staggered to the raft at last and fumbled in the food pouch for dried meat. She felt hollow with hunger, for she had burned energy at a mad rate on this first day. Katharine knew she must eat far more than she wanted before setting out, every time, if she would last through each day's ordeal. And that would mean stopping to resupply her store more often than she had hoped.

The edge of the moon was creeping into view beyond the cliff-top, lending its silver light to the river. "I'd better lie up and rest a bit," she said aloud, feeling her voice grate in her throat, sounding strange for lack of regular use.

"This little river ought to be a natural place to catch small game—or even antelope, if I had a gun to shoot them with." She sighed, thinking of red meat, tender between her teeth, the rich juices slipping down her throat to lend her body energy.

"But rabbit will do," she added, as she recalled the many times a skinny hare had saved her from starvation. Snares were easy to make, and she had saved ligament and strips of hide for just such use.

Chewing a stiff strip of dried rattlesnake meat, Katharine leaned back against the cliff and closed her eyes again. The meat softened as she chewed, sipping from time to time from a cupped hand held beneath a trickle of water down the wall behind her.

When she had rested a bit more, she rose and began to set her snares, though the climb up the rocky stream-bed tried her aching body. She would live if she could, but now she realized that she was too tired and battered and discouraged to resent death, if it came.

She slept, at last, lying on top of her improvised bedding, too exhausted to cover herself. When she woke, the sky was silver, and a clump of clouds, touched now with pink and gold, edged the canyon rim. She lay still, watching the sunrise brighten the strip of sky above her rocky cove, feeling as if she could lie there peacefully and drift into a sleep that might never end. Yet she still had some unexplainable drive to live, and her snares were waiting to be checked.

She sat up, grabbing her back with both hands and feeling the long aches in her shoulders and wrists. Remembering old injuries from her horse training days, she knew she must work the pain out of her bones or she might not be able to control the raft down another treacherous stretch of the Snake.

There was no more dried snake-meat, so she stretched her bones as well as she could and climbed up the rocky angles of the overgrown ravine to see if she had caught something overnight. The first snare was tripped, but nothing remained but a wisp of anonymous gray fur. The next was undisturbed.

Katharine's stomach was growling now, and her knees felt a bit wobbly as she searched through a tangle of sagebrush near the top of the cliff for her last snare. It held something, for she could see it jerking before she came up far enough to know what it held. One furious eye was visible, the rest of the animal being curled tightly around itself, hind paws scrabbling at the thong that held it suspended from a low bush.

A weasel? Maybe, she thought, though she wasn't familiar with the critters in this area. Not a tasty meal, she thought, but she took out her hunting knife and knocked the creature in the head with the horn handle. It was bigger than she thought, she found as she cut its throat and took it back down into the shade of the cove.

The fur was handsome, once she shook the dust from it, but the meat was scanty. She built a small fire, using the dry twigs and branches caught among the rocks along the wash, and spitted the carcass on a long branch of green cottonwood. She set rocks around the fire to focus the heat and secured the spit with more rocks to hold the meat steady over the flames.

Before long, moisture began to sizzle on the stones, and the smell of cooking flesh filled the little cove. Katharine watched it closely—it wouldn't do to lose her meal, for she hadn't the energy left to hunt for more. Stretching her legs and easing her sore shoulders, she waited patiently for the weasel to cook. Before it blackened, she took the lean carcass off the spit and laid it to cool on a clean rock. When it was edible, she dug in, finding it tough and stringy, strong-flavored but chewable.

She ate it all, for there wasn't enough to replenish her energy otherwise, and then she lay back to watch the sunlight slip along the canyon beyond the mouth of the cove. Here the river ran from east to west, and the light strengthened until the water shone and the wall beyond it glimmered with dancing reflections.

She slept for a long while, and when she woke she realized that the wobbly feeling had left her, though she was still terribly sore and stiff. Before the day grew even hotter, she tried to do some running in place, stretching and bending to loosen herself into usable condition.

She wanted to rest here for a day or so, but she knew she must move. If she could catch some more animals, of whatever kind, she could continue her journey.

Not only was there the danger of pursuit behind her, but if she arrived too late, the mountains she must cross to get to Oregon might be deep in snow. She had no equipment to help her survive the bitter cold she might find there.

When the sun warmed the cove, she found herself feeling better, and she moved up the dry channel again, resetting her snares. As she neared the top, she heard a familiar sound, the dry rasp of rattles. A big rattlesnake was just what she needed, and now she knew she was able to cope with one.

Katharine backed down the wash to find her discarded stick she had used for a spit. Securing her knife to the thick end, she crept up the slope again, watching her step carefully, for it was now hot enough for snakes to be active.

She stopped before she reached the level at which she had heard the rattle and searched the ground among the brittle sage. The mottled coils were hard to spot against the equally mottled grit and the stiff gray droppings from the sage, but once she spotted it she pitched a rock off to the right. The rattler struck blindly at the motion, and she severed its head with one quick slice of the razor-sharp knife, while remaining well out of range.

She had never thought of herself as a savage, before that moment. As she lifted the snake and the blood dripped from the raw neck, Katharine was seized by voracious hunger. She ripped the round body open with the blade and pulled out strips of bloody meat, eating it raw, letting the blood run down her chin.

She dropped to sit on a clear patch of gravel while she devoured the snake, leaving only the skin. Once she was sated, she stared down at the red-stained spine and almost vomited. That would have been terribly wasteful, however, so she held herself very still until her stomach settled.

Then she rolled up the skin and made her careful way back down to the raft. Now the sun shone full upon the cove and her small pile of improvised supplies.

It was time to move, while she was filled with meat.

When she stopped again, she was certain there would be no shortage of snakes, and if she had to live on those, she would. Taking the time only to scrub out the skin with water, then with sand, then with grit, she tied the length to the pack thongs and washed herself in the edge of the water. Then she checked the ties securing her hard-won supplies to the biggest log in the raft and pushed the clumsy craft out into the relatively still water of the cove.

Climbing aboard, she shook away the wet like a dog and steered the slow raft toward the current out in the river. That caught her again and the raft turned at her urging to charge, once again, headlong down the river toward whatever destiny waited for it.

CHAPTER FIFTEEN

The country west of the Tetons soon proved to be every bit as rough as Sun-Shot had expected. Soon even Murray admitted they needed to find a route that wouldn't risk breaking the horses' fragile legs, and they turned back south toward the river.

"Up ahead, three-four days ride, there's lava fields that look like the outskirts of hell," he told One-Ear. "Brittle, black stuff—looks like when your Ma made candy and it bubbled up and hardened. Over yonder...."—he pointed north toward the bleak brown mountains—"...must've been the volcanoes that belched up that witch's broth. It's no country for man or beast.

"I talked to a scout who went that way with one of the Oregon-bound caravans. It was hell on animals, people, and death on wagon wheels. If that girl is walking through that country, she may not come out alive on the other side. I hope you take note of that, if we don't find any trace of her later."

Murray grunted and spat as O'Neill dismounted to lead his horse and the pack animal carefully southward. It was afternoon, and the sun into which they had been traveling blazed mercilessly down on the rock to the west. Even now Sun-Shot could see occasional arms of lava that had extended this far from the parent mountains. What lay farther west, he didn't want to know firsthand.

They angled southward, crossing the arid land, the

rough outcrops of lava, and the long stretches of nothing much in particular. The river, when they came to it, lay below cliffs too steep to descend, so they moved along the winding course until they found a wash leading downward. At its bottom grew a clump of cottonwoods and willows, small and stunted but offering a bit of wood and shelter from the merciless sun.

They paused there to camp, for the horses were beginning to flag. Goldie was limping as he came to a halt, and Sun-Shot unsaddled him and led him into a shallow eddy to soak his weary legs. The horse snorted in the chilly water, but as the coolness eased his sore hoof he seemed to relax, letting his ears droop and snuffling softly through his velvet nostrils.

Sun-Shot waded out and rubbed him down with a wad of dried grass, talking to him softly all the while. The gelding closed his eyes and sighed, shifting his weight to the other foot and raising his hoof for his master to inspect.

There was a chip of rock wedged between hoof and shoe. Sun-Shot drew his knife from its sheath and carefully pried the painful stone free; Goldie shook his hide and looked toward the river bank, where the other horses were grazing on the tufts of sun-scorched grass growing along the base of the cliff.

Murray stood there, frowning at his guide. "Why'n hell you put that horse ahead of everything else I don't know. Here I am, tired out and hungry and ready to rest a bit, and you're out there babying that animal. We need a fire and some cooked food, for a change."

O'Neill waded out of the water, sat on a protruding rock, and pulled off his boots. "There's plenty of dry wood over there against the bank, where the water left it when it went down," he said. "If you are as hungry as you think, you might be getting some together so I can strike a light when I get through here." He emptied the water from his boots and set them aside to dry.

"If you had the brains God gave a goose," he said to his employer, "you'd know that we get only as far as our horses can go. After that, if they play out, we walk, and that means we'll never catch up with that girl, if she's still alive and moving."

Murray looked puzzled for a moment, and Sun-Shot found himself wondering just how stupid the man actually was. He kept discovering unsuspected new depths to Murray's lack of knowledge and judgment. Sighing, he rose and hobbled over the rough ground in his socked feet to the pile of debris that offered fuel for a fire. In five minutes, he had arranged a pyramid of twigs and branches, struck fire into tinder from his flint and steel, and was blowing on a tentative blaze.

The sun was down behind the cliff wall, and the chill of the desert night soon would envelop them. The warmth was a comfort, and soon the smell of jerky boiling in his small pot, along with a handful of wild sage, filled the air. Coffee was bubbling in the blackened coffee pot, as well, and when the two sat down to eat hot food for the first time in days, Sun-Shot found himself feeling almost friendly toward One-Ear.

When he'd swilled out the coffeepot with water and scrubbed the stew pot with sand, he sat with his back to his saddle and stared across the fire at Murray. "You know, Mr. Murray," he said, "I just don't understand why you're spendin' all this time and money hunting for a woman who doesn't want you. You don't seem to understand that an unhappy woman can make your life miserable."

Murray looked shocked. "A woman? You're crazy, O'Neill. My Daddy said no woman ever born had enough sense to come in out of the rain. How could she make me miserable?"

Sun-Shot shook his head. "Your Daddy was dead wrong, and unless he was dead stupid, he knew it. You said he used to beat your Mama. What did she do about that?"

"Nothing. Nothing at all. He used to sleep out in the barn, sometimes, just to keep from having to look at her, he said, but she didn't do one solitary thing."

"Except kick him out of his bedroom. I wonder how she managed that? Did they keep a gun in that room?" O'Neill asked.

"Of course they did, but she'd never have dared threaten Pa with it."

Sun-Shot grinned. "I wouldn't want to bet on that." He rose and pushed the fire together, unrolled his blanket, and lay down with his head pillowed on the saddle. From time to time he chuckled, thinking of poor dumb One-Ear, thinking his Mama couldn't punish his father for his cruelty. Even a timid woman had weapons to use against a man, and one who wasn't timid was dangerous as a sow bear, when she had reason to be.

Now Sun-Shot was moving by guess and instinct. There was no trace of anything that would indicate their quarry might have passed this way. If she was on foot, she might have passed without leaving any sign, and in this vast country there was no way to know what route she had chosen. As it was, however, Sun-Shot wondered if she might not choose to follow the river closely, for even if she had secured a large water skin there was no way for a person afoot to carry enough water to last through a long desert crossing. No, if he were in her shoes he would stay as close to the river as possible.

From time to time he followed a cut in the canyon wall down which he could ride or clamber. Murray grumbled, of course, at the delay, but even he understood that without some clue to indicate Katharine's passing they were moving blind.

Mounted as they were, they could cover distance fairly quickly, for the presence of the river meant their horses had plenty of water. Though the heat of summer had withered the grass, there was quite a lot along the edges of the canyon, so the mounts were in good shape, able to sustain the long effort demanded of them. Because of that, Sun-Shot was not worried that the woman was getting impossibly far ahead of them. Yet something niggled at his mind; what was he overlooking?

He had ridden Goldie down an easy approach to the river, where the cliffs were low and a runnel cut through them to make it even easier. Leading the pack animal and followed by a muttering Murray, who had learned to keep his cursing unintelligible, he dismounted before reaching the river and examined the ground closely as he neared the water.

A path ran along the edge of the stream, showing signs of occasional flooding but so deeply worn into the rocky verge that it was obviously very old. Probably an animal track, Sun-Shot thought, but also quite likely used by any tribe that passed this way on hunting expeditions. There was, however, no trace of a moccasin or boot track. If Katharine was taking this route, she had either concealed her passage extremely well or was on the other side of the river.

Still, if she had come so far without dying and had not chosen to go by way of the Bitterroots, it stood to reason that someone so tough and determined would do the logical thing. That was to follow the river, which gave both guidance to one who wanted to go northwestward, if that was her goal, and water to keep her alive.

As long as the waterside path offered space for the horses, he followed it, but at last he could see ahead a point at which a buttress of stone thrust out into the river, blocking their trail. At the first break in the canyon wall he led his group up and out onto the desert again. The spicy scent of the sage was strong in his nostrils, after the wet stone smell of the canyon.

"How long do we keep goin' this way without knowin'

what we're doin'?" Murray asked. He turned his head to gaze over the long swells of sage-dotted country, dry and unwelcoming and deadly to the unwary.

"Until we find some sign or you decide to give up and go home," Sun-Shot replied.

Murray looked thoughtful. That pleased his guide. Even if he had to go back and return the money, he'd find some way to support his family. He found himself wishing that One-Ear would choose that option, for he was sick to death of this unwelcome task.

CHAPTER SIXTEEN

Struggling with the sweep to control her raft was wearing her down to the bone, Katharine knew. It was almost impossible to find enough to eat—she had finished her dried meat and had to stop, every time the river permitted that, to set traps and to hunt for snakes, lizards, and rabbits. Yet such small creatures could not rebuild her strength for the difficult task of steering her craft past the dangers of the river, and she realized she must stop for long enough to find larger game. That entailed spotting a possible landing while she was far enough upstream to steer the raft to shore.

As it took all her attention to steer clear of the boulders that had fallen from the cliffs into the middle of the river, she found it more than difficult to find a place to land. Though in midsummer the water level was relatively low, the river still ran with terrible power, and the stress was wearing her beyond enduring. When she spotted a patch of green in one wall of the canyon, almost a mile ahead, she put all her strength into angling the sweep so as to guide the raft into the mouth of a stream running out of a cleft in the cliff. That formed a small cove, where cottonwoods and willows grew in the soil that had washed down from the plain above.

When she had the raft well into the calm water and had tied it to one of the willows, Katharine took no time to eat or drink. She dropped onto the ground and fell asleep instantly.

She woke to darkness and knew she had slept for hours. Only when the glare of the moon peered over the cliff-top did she have some idea of the time, though even that was a guess, for so winding was the route of the Snake that the sun and moon seldom rose over the cliffs at the same angle.

Katharine had learned, during her journey, that clocks and calendars were irrelevant to survival; the idea would have upset her mother, who had structured her life by the hands of the big clock Pa had bought her as a wedding present. Yet there was something liberating in leaving behind any regard for time as marked by clocks.

Stiff and sore from her efforts, she stretched her legs, moved her shoulders, and finally rose to stand looking down at the water that swirled around her raft. With a sigh, she bent and washed her face and arms, then waded in and washed herself from hair to heels. Her wet pants and the remnants of her buckskin shirt she hung in a willow tree to dry as she examined her skimpy possessions.

The coil of hide rope she had twisted would provide makings for rabbit traps, and that would help, but she needed something stronger. Another badger would be all right, rank as the meat might taste, but she preferred an antelope, if possible. She had seen the distinctively marked animals drinking along the river as she volleyed past. They were not nearly as large as the elk she had killed, but, as she lacked a gun, a smaller animal would be easier to kill. It was time for her to supply her needs while she had the strength to do it. She wrapped herself in her skin blanket, securing it at her waist with a length of her rope.

Making sure that the raft was securely fastened, she turned to move up the small stream that had cut a ravine through the canyon rim. She went slowly along the creek, watching the damp soil at the edge of the water. Occasionally she saw a track of a bird or some tiny beast too small to be of use. As she followed the stream it became swifter, for it descended rapidly to the level of the river. As she crept around a sharp angle, she found the space between the stony walls wider than she had expected. At last she came to a spot from which she could see the origin of the stream, a hole in the rock from which gushed a spring, which evidently had its source in some underground river.

To her right, across the stream, she saw a trail worn into the rock, very narrow, very steep, and she thought that might be the place where larger animals from the plain above might come down to drink. She hiked up her robe and waded across the narrow but rapid current. As she neared the track she could see marks that hinted at the passing of small, sharp hooves. The track was so narrow it promised the chance to lie in wait here below, and use a rope to grab a descending animal as it stepped out into the ravine. Her knife, even sharper now from long use and continual whetting against stone, would shorten the struggle, for she would cut the beast's throat.

To her delight, there were cat-tails growing at the edges of the creek. Before working out the details of her plan to get meat, she dug up the roots of several and carried them back to her raft, where her flint and steel would provide fire to kindle some of the dried drift that had accumulated in the cove. Once she had her fire going, she rummaged among her painfully gathered supplies, trimming edges off the larger hides to reinforce her twisted rope. It would be no small task to catch and hold an antelope long enough to kill it.

She had buried her roots beneath the fire, and by the time she was satisfied with her lines they had roasted well. Though they didn't give her the strength that meat would, they did fill her stomach and ease the growling of her gut. An oversized but incautious lizard provided a bit of meat, as well, so that when she rose to begin creating her snare she had a bit more energy than she had expected.

Gathering her rope into a coil, checking the edge of her knife, Katharine shouldered her equipment and trudged back up the creek to the slot in the ravine wall. Now, reinforced by her meal, she had the energy to examine it closely. She hesitated to venture up it, for she had no idea how sensitive an antelope's sense of smell might be. Warning her prey off with her own scent would be a disaster that might spell the end of her.

Instead, she searched the adjacent wall until she found an irregular slope she felt she could manage to climb. She dropped her burden into a cranny and set her feet into cracks in the stone wall, reaching high for others to accommodate her fingers. The ravine had been cut through stone and soil, and it was relatively stable. Ignoring the pain of scraped fingers, she moved upward, her progress slow but steady.

Before she got to the top, she could hear the faint rattle of hooves on the stony soil of the plain. It might, she thought, be a small buffalo herd. It might also be some group of Indians, who at this time of the year might be indulging in a last hunt before moving toward their winter campsite.

Before taking the chance of thrusting her head above the level of the soil, she eased one eye over the edge, head tilted so as to make it less visible. At first she could see nothing except the stems of stiff, dry grass and clumps of sage. Then something moved in the distance, and she saw a horse, another, a line of them, most dragging travois. This was a tribe moving its location, she realized, for there were many women, bending beneath packs, as well as children following amid a clutter of dogs. All were quiet, which told her that this was a country where they did not feel safe enough to risk talk and laughter. Even the dogs traveled silently, without a bark or a whimper to betray them.

Kate drew her head back and waited until there was no

reverberation of hoof on rocky soil. When a last she risked her eye above the edge again she found nothing on the plain. Then she climbed out of the ravine and stood, stretching the tension out of her bones.

Bending, she searched the dry soil for tracks, and they were there. A dim trail led from the mouth of the track into the ravine, off toward the dry brown hills in the distance. The antelope would come, she knew, when night hid them from any predators that might lurk on the plain.

That was fine, for she, the worst predator, would be waiting below.

CHAPTER SEVENTEEN

There was no use, Sun-Shot decided, in continuing to wander along the Snake River Canyon, without knowing whether or not their quarry was ahead or behind. He faced Murray with that conclusion early one morning.

"I think we'd do best to cut across country and catch the river a lot farther downstream. She's got to stick close to the water, but we have pack animals and plenty of water skins, so we can afford to cut off a lot of miles. If she's anywhere along the Snake, we should be able to intercept her along her route. That is, if luck is with us.

Murray squinted and spat. He didn't speak for some time. Then he nodded reluctantly and began saddling his horse. Well, that was an improvement. Anything that didn't make One-Ear curse had to be agreeable to him.

The silence was so welcome that Sun-Shot did nothing to disturb it. Instead he clucked to Goldie, once they got under way, and he set a rapid pace toward the northwest, avoiding the intricate loops of the river. They could make thirty or forty miles today, he figured, if nothing happened to delay them. But of course something did.

Not for nothing had O'Neill spent his youth among the Cheyenne. He could sense the presence of potential enemies before any overt sign came clear, and before noon he felt a prickle along his spine that warned of something ahead. They had been walking and leading the animals, but now he remounted. Head up, he sniffed the wind before murmuring to Murray, "Something in the wind. Take care, and keep your eyes open. Watch your animal's ears. If they begin to twitch, get off and hold his nose in your hands to keep him from whinnying. I'll tend to the pack animal, and Goldie knows better than to sound off."

Murray opened his mouth to protest, but a glare choked him off. His face turned red, but as that made no noise Sun-Shot had no objection.

They moved forward quietly for some time, but at last the guide signaled a halt. "I think I'll do a bit of scouting," he said softly. "You wait here. Do not build a fire to make coffee. Do not go wandering around inspecting the landscape. Do not let the horses get away. Tie them to that rock over there and sit down on it yourself."

As he slipped away over the rocky ground, Sun-Shot congratulated himself. He seemed to have finally quelled Murray's habit of arguing.

Then he concentrated his mind upon his task. If his trained senses and his instincts were not at fault, there were people moving on the plain. At this time he doubted they would be white men, and if they were Indians, the odds were that they would not be friendly. With that in mind, he crept over the rough ground like a lizard, feeling in the rocky soil the vibrations of hooves and footsteps. Not distant, now, but drawing nearer.

Blending with the hummocky ground, taking advantage of the cover of many rounded boulders, Sun-Shot waited for the travelers to come into his range of vision. He had learned patience from his Cheyenne companions, and he did not fidget as he took advantage of the present inactivity to rest. His senses remained alert, and in time he could hear the sounds of horses. Risking one eye over the nearest round rock, he saw, amid a mist of dust, a tribal group on the move.

Their direction was roughly parallel to the course of the river, though at some distance from the canyon, and the slow pace told him that both the very old and the very young accompanied the group. Though they were distant, he could tell that the horses were weary, and the people walked with more determination than energy. If he and Murray stayed in place or diverted their course even farther from the river, they should be able to avoid any chance of confrontation.

He waited, silent and watchful, until the line of travelers disappeared in the distance. When he returned to Murray he found the man pacing up and down beside the horses, chewing on his dingy moustache and muttering under his breath. As Sun-Shot approached, One-Ear turned and barked, "When we goin' to get on our way? Been wastin' time, lettin' that woman run free and thumb her nose at me. We got to go right now!"

"No," said the guide in a peaceable voice. "We've got Indians up ahead. It's best to keep clear of them. I don't know what tribe they belong to, and whatever it is there's no knowing how they'll react to white men. We got lucky once, and there's no use tempting Providence. We can rest the horses for a day, and that will be nothing but good, anyway."

Murray roared like an animal, his face turning turkey-wattle red. "Be damned if I do! You lazy bastard, you just want to loll around 'stead of doin' your job."

For a moment Sun-Shot thought the man was going to try to hit him, and he prepared to lay him low, but Murray thought better of his impulse.

"You want to risk your hair again a-purpose?" Sun-Shot asked. "We woke up, if you recall, looking up at warriors who had the drop on us, and we got out of that by pure-d luck. Now we've got the chance to steer clear of Indian trouble, and you want to go charging off and chance having our luck change? I don't think so!"

"Why not bushwhack 'em?" Murray growled. "Surely two white men with plenty of ammunition can wipe out a bunch of scurvy redskins!"

O'Neill stared at him with undisguised contempt. "You want to kill a bunch of women and children? This isn't a war party, Murray; it's a whole clan moving to a new site, with very few warriors and hunters with them. Those are probably off looking for game. Old folks, babies, dogs, everything they've got travels to the new campsite. You may be a cold-blooded killer, but I wasn't raised that way. I tell you plain, here and now, that if you make a move to do something like that I'll kill you and never think twice about it."

The man turned away and stalked toward his bedroll, where he dug out a twist of tobacco and began to chew it savagely, spitting viciously at a tuft of dead grass. Well fine, the guide thought. Let him act like a two-year-old. Better than acting like a fiend, that was for sure.

Sun-Shot led the horses to a fresh patch of grass and hobbled them. He might as well get some rest, which had been pretty scanty of late. You'd best catch up on your sleep, he said to Murray. I'm going to.

* * * * * * *

He was wearier than he thought, for he fell asleep almost at once, though as usual he kept some part of himself alert for danger. When he woke it was with a sudden feeling that something was wrong. He sat and looked first to the horses. Goldie was cropping grass lazily, evidently enjoying his rest. The pack horse stood beyond his mount, heel cocked, head drooping, dozing in the sun. But where was Murray's mount?

Where, by God, was Murray?

O'Neill shot to his feet and looked around, but there was no sign of the man or his horse, though his pack and bedroll were still in place. Dammit! Why couldn't the idiot do what he was told? He'd rather take care of twin idiots,

Sun-Shot decided, than somebody like this easterner. How the man had managed to sneak out without waking him was a conundrum.

The track was easy to find, of course, as Murray might have learned how to find a track but had never mastered the concept of concealing his own trail. It led off in the direction from which the guide had returned from his reconnaissance earlier. Now the sun was well down in the west, and soon those travelers would be making their night camp, never suspecting that a madman might be stalking them.

Muttering some colorful Cheyenne observations on Murray's ancestors and personal habits, O'Neill packed up camp, saddled Goldie, and led him and the pack horse along his employer's route. He hoped devoutly that he would catch him in time, before he roused some tribe to bloodshed. One-Ear might think himself a mighty warrior, but he was a coward of the worst kind, preferring just the sort of prey this group represented, for he had no idea that Indian women and children would fight like demons, when the need arose.

Sun-Shot chuckled. Women and children might sound like easy pickings to someone like Murray, with his inaccurate idea of their capabilities, but the guide knew such people. If they were as helpless as Murray thought, the menfolk would never have left them to travel alone.

CHAPTER EIGHTEEN

Kathleen explored the ravine with care, noting every possible hummock that might trip her as she struggled with her prey, every rock or root that might impede her hunt. She peered up the slit in the ravine wall as far as possible, then she climbed the wall again and looked down into the track from above, committing to her memory every angle and slant of it. Knowing how the critter had come might possibly help her to catch it.

Once she had her plan of campaign firmly in mind, she decided the best thing to do would be to rest that afternoon, so as to be as strong as possible for her efforts that night. She returned down the ravine to the raft, where she laid out her patched-together blanket on the ground in the shade of one of the willows. As she stretched out she saw something burrowing into the damp soil beside the water. She rolled toward the spot and dug with her fingers after it, pulling out of the ground a dirt-colored insect almost the size of her hand.

Its body was covered with grit, so she carried it to the water and rinsed it as clean as possible. She had learned long since that most insects could be eaten; by now, if one happened to kill her she didn't much care. She pulled off its legs and peeled away the chitin before scrunching it up. There was more to it than she had expected and she fell asleep with her hunger somewhat satisfied. Because of that she slept more deeply than she expected, waking when the sun was behind the cliff and the air began to cool.

Time to be up and doing! She whetted her knife once more, just to make sure it was keen. She had left her coil of rope in the ravine, ready to hand, and unfortunately there was little else she could use in her hunting. The old Hawken—she sighed and forgot it. There was no time or energy to waste on what might have been.

She was settled into her hiding place before the sun was altogether down. As darkness enveloped the ravine, she honed all her senses to detect any movement along the narrow slot in its wall. Putting herself into waiting mode, she thought, with one part of her mind, of herself as she had been a scant two months before, impatient, unaware, wondering when a real life might begin for her. That girl seemed like a stranger to her as she was now, taught by stress and danger to attend to every breath of wind over rocks, every scuttle of insect or reptile over the gritty soil. She could even hear the dim rush of the river, dulled though it was by distance and the bends in the ravine.

She owed much to the difficulties of her life, she realized. The hard work had given her strength of body; her struggles to maintain the ranch as long as her father had need of it had given her strength of will. Perhaps most of all she owed to her mother, who had given her not only much of her own knowledge but also the friendship with the Shoshone woman that had resulted in such valuable training concerning survival in the wild. If she survived— if she managed to reach her kin in Oregon—it would be directly attributable to that training.

Relaxing against the wall of the ravine, she re-examined her arrangement of rope that formed the snare she hoped to fill with the struggling body of an antelope. Secured to tough shrubs on either side of the track, the lines would hamper the animal long enough for her to cut its throat with her knife. If they didn't, she might well be sliced to ribbons by the sharp hooves of her quarry.

In her many weeks of travel and danger, she had learned to wait, not the least of her new skills. It was as well, for the sun was long down behind the cliffs and night was thick in the ravine before the faintest tickle of sound clicked, deep in the track. Katharine was on her feet, swiftly, soundlessly, drawing the lines just tightly enough so she could snap them into place as the animal emerged from its secret entryway.

It almost worked.

The antelope came faster than she had expected and was partially through before the jerked up the ropes. Missing the front legs, still the lines tangled in the back ones, throwing the beast off-balance. It scrambled for footing, and, realizing she had only one chance to gain her goal, Kate tackled the antelope from one side, gripped it around the neck with her left arm and used her knife with the right. As she stabbed it, the creature returned the favor, jabbing a hoof into her thigh, but she hardly felt the pain, knowing that her life depended upon making this kill.

The animal spasmed as the blade sliced through its neck. She found herself riding it as it bucked and squirmed, while bleeding its life out onto the floor of the ravine. Using her weight to burden her prey, she clung onto him for dear life. That was entirely true, for she would have no energy for another effort, if this one did not succeed. The draining task of steering the raft had used her body almost to the bone, and now she was losing a lot of blood. Yet even as her strength drained into the grit of the ravine, she still dug in with the knife and held on.

The dying took a long time. When at last the antelope dropped to its knees and its head drooped to the ground, it gave only a last shudder, a quiver, and Katharine loosed her hold and fell beside her kill. Only when it ceased did she realize that the creature had been bleating all the while it was dying, probably alarming every living thing within miles. But now it made no difference.

Katharine sat for a long time in the darkness, panting, while she tore loose some of the last thongs from her shirt and bound them around her leg to stop the bleeding. Then she crawled to the edge of the stream and dug handfuls of mud to plaster over the spot where the sharp hoof had stabbed. After that, she knew she must replenish her body. To do that she had to crawl back to the dead animal and cut off enough meat to provide a bit of energy. She washed the blood from her knife, finding that she had dulled it a bit.

Katharine felt about for a stone suitable for whetting its edge. When she found one she spent valuable time honing her blade. Then she fumbled her way back and found the animal, as much by its smell as by memory. Feeling to locate the haunch, she pierced the tough hide with the point of her knife and worried loose a chunk of meat, which she devoured, raw and bloody and grateful to her belly. She could feel energy building in her body as she chewed and swallowed.

Before dawn she had recovered enough strength to begin skinning out the game, which was a hard job if one was fresh and filled with energy. Still, she persisted, drawing loose the hide, removing the guts and saving the stomach to use as a bag for water or other necessities, and cutting the meat into manageable chunks.

By mid-morning she had saved out all the ligament, the usable gut, and the bones that could be sharpened into tools. She rolled it all into the hide, with the meat, and dragged the awkward bundle toward the river and her raft.

* * * * * * *

Her leg had stiffened, though the bleeding had stopped, and it took a long while to reach her goal. Once there, she used her flint and steel to kindle a fire, using dry driftwood she had left ready, and roasted more of the meat.

147

She ate carefully, knowing that too much food at this point would make her ill, but she rested and ate small bits at intervals for the rest of the day. There would be time tomorrow to begin curing the hide and slicing the meat to dry.

She woke with fever, as she had expected; she peeled off bark from a willow tree and found a water-hollowed stone into which she dropped hot stones until the water boiled to make tea. Meanwhile she began to dry thin slices of meat before the fire, which she kept burning at a good rate. Dizzy and weak, she sipped the tea from the stone, lapping it like a dog, and it helped.

When her thigh began to swell with infection, she knew she must cauterize the wound. That was not a thought that brought her any comfort. It was hard enough to do that for a sufferer who was held down by his kin, his wits somewhat dimmed with liquor. To do it to herself, in cold blood, was not something she looked forward to. Sitting in the shade of the willows, she reflected, with fever-driven logic, on her alternatives.

If I wanted to die, she thought, I've had plenty of chances. So I must want to live, for some odd reason. She drew a deep breath, trying to clear her woozy head. "I'm not going to get any clearer," she said aloud. "If I wait I may forget entirely what I must do, and then I will die. Sounds inviting, actually." She jerked herself upright.

Without further thought, she crawled to the fire and thrust the blade of her knife into the coals. While it heated, she laid out her blanket on the ground, settled herself on it, her back against a willow, and extended her leg, moaning faintly with the pain.

She reached for the bone handle of the knife, her hand padded with a bit of rabbit fur, and drew the blade out of the coals. Without time for thinking, she jabbed the red-hot point into the festered wound and screamed long and loud as pus spurted and blood ran. Then she passed out, leaving the knife-blade embedded in her flesh.

CHAPTER NINETEEN

Sun-Shot rode wide of Murray's tracks, but he could see that the idiot was heading as straight as he could figure toward the last known locations of the group the guide had seen. Did he think he could ride into a file of Shoshone, or whatever tribe they belonged to, and grab him a woman just because he wanted one? Sun-Shot had seen the glint in One-Ear's eyes when he mentioned the bunch being mostly women and children. He should have known better than to go to sleep and leave his half-witted charge unsupervised.

Now he swung wide of the route he had guessed at, but he didn't rush the horses. He knew the quarry could feel hoofbeats through the ground beneath their feet even better than he could, himself. No use alerting them to the fact that One-Ear wasn't alone. That did not mean that he dallied, however, for he could walk as fast as any horse and proceeded to prove it. He made good time in a great curve on a course to intersect the tribe's line of march.

From time to time Sun-Shot paused to lie flat on the ground, ear to the soil, listening for the distant thud of hooves. Dim but distinct, at last he heard the sound of a horse...galloping? Surely even One-Ear wouldn't attack a file of strange Indians as if he were charging a ladies' tea party?

Discarding his cautious methods, O'Neill mounted Goldie, kicked him into a trot, and, followed by the pack horse, took off for the direction from which he had heard the hooves. He didn't know what he would find when he got there, but he felt an obligation to learn what was happening with Murray. One thing was certain; he was not going to attack a bunch of non-hostile Indians on behalf of a certifiable lunatic.

He heard yells and war cries long before he came in sight of the confused conflict. Ground-hitching Goldie and the pack horse, O'Neill crept forward under cover of the thick growth of sage until he could distinguish the combatants. Cursing the lack of the good binoculars he used to have as an Army scout, he focused on the tangle of shapes amid the dust some quarter of a mile from his position.

Murray's bellowed curses were unmistakable. The shrill cries of the furious women and the whoops of the few elderly warriors punctuated the strange chorus. For a moment it looked like the worst dog fight he had ever encountered, but then it began to resolve itself, as the central figure went down and most of the women backed away. Sun-Shot grunted as he saw that one single woman had been left to deal with the intruder into their journey.

He could read the story as clearly as if he were on the spot. Murray had gone roaring in, snatched that very angry woman out of the line of marchers and tried to ride off with her. She had evidently resisted with all her might, which with a woman of her kind was surprisingly great, until her fellow travelers had time to come to her aid. They had pulled down One-Ear's horse; the beast was still standing, quivering and terrified, his reins held by a small boy. Then he knew they had subdued its rider, and now the woman he had attacked was given the honor of punishing him. This left Sun-Shot with a dilemma of conscience. He had contracted to find Murray's woman for him. That now seemed to be a moot question, as Murray was clearly about to die. Did he owe the man his life, in return for a handful of gold pieces?

150

Not even his godly parents' training could convince him of that. No, he couldn't find it moral or acceptable to attack a bunch of women and children to save a man who meant them nothing but harm. He did feel that he should remain in place, however, as a sort of duty.

Then O'Neill admitted to himself that he would enjoy seeing that animal suffer at the hands of women, whom he had done nothing but denigrate and insult. Murray owed this death to Murray's mother and to the people and animals he had abused and killed, and perhaps, more than anything, to the woman he had bought. During the weeks and weeks of following her, Sun-Shot had come to respect her, both as a person and as a survivor. He owed it to her to describe the last hours of the life of her pursuer, however painful it might be to watch, if he ever caught up with her and got the chance.

Before the thing was done, Sun-Shot was grateful for the distance between him and the scene on the plain. He had wondered what the angry people would do, what method they would choose for punishing their attacker. Lacking a ready source of wood, they might have forgone the use of fire, but they were people of limitless inventiveness. The dried sagebrush around them, scanty though it seemed, provided fuel enough for their purposes.

He sat and rested while children ran back and forth gathering armfuls of the prickly stuff. There was no use in paying close attention to the preparations, for it would be difficult enough to see the use to which that fire would be put. Glancing toward the busy group from time to time, he waited until the process was well under way before he focused his attention upon it.

He had watched, as a teenaged boy, the Cheyenne entertain an enemy captive, his youthful emotions strangely excited by the experience. Later, he had seen this again, this time with the horror that maturity had brought to his conscience. The applications of fire to the extremities, of blades to the skin and live coals to the scalp, making the brain boil, were not unfamiliar to him, but the fact that he knew the sufferer, however wicked he had been, made this somehow worse.

It seemed to take forever, and Murray's screams reached him entirely too clearly. Those, thankfully, grew weaker with time, and Sun-Shot realized that the travelers were in a hurry—too much of one to take their usual leisurely way with this captive. While One-Ear would never know or appreciate it, he was lucky that his pain was relatively short-lived. Even so, his dying seemed to O'Neill to last forever. He thought he could smell the stink of blood and spilled guts, though the distance was really too great for that to be true. Before all was done, Sun-Shot realized that no one, even Murray, deserved to die at the hands of those women, although they had, he knew, a very legitimate grudge against him.

By the time the screams were quenched and the travelers had proceeded upon their trek, O'Neill felt almost as if he had been the focus of their attention, himself. He hurt, physically, as if his own nerves and bones somehow echoed the other's travail. Somehow he dragged himself up onto Goldie and began to move from his present position.

He felt both sorrowful and nauseated, and at last he stopped Goldie and leaned over to vomit onto the plain. He dismounted for long enough to rinse his mouth and wipe his forehead, but something kept him moving along, though he shortened the route he had planned out to take him and Murray to the Snake.

He couldn't have said why, but he felt an obligation to that woman he had trailed so long. She needed to know that her pursuer was dead, that there was no reason to flee with such caution and speed toward whatever goal she had set for herself. He had taken a role in her trouble, and his conscience told him that he owed her that much. Even, perhaps, some time and help in finding her way.

When he had recovered his normal balance, the guide kicked Goldie into a faster walk and headed toward the river, knowing the Indians who had put paid to One-Ear were moving westward along its course. He would head directly toward the stream, which from his present position was somewhat south of west. Refreshed by their long wait, the horses moved easily and without tiring for a long time. By the time they were ready for a rest, the long dark streak that was the canyon was visible in the distance.

When he was within a couple of miles of the river, he dismounted and led the animals, making a smaller image for anyone watching to detect against the pale sagebrush of the plain. There was relatively little cover, should any danger appear, but Sun-Shot took advantage of clumps of sagebrush and piles of rocks, rounded boulders deposited there by some long-past flooding of the stream. This caused some delay, but he reached the rim of the canyon safely and stared down at last into its depths.

Here the Snake ran deep between stony cliffs, and from time to time a trickle of water from some spring flowed from a crack or a hole and shone as it flowed downward to join the river below. There was no sign of anyone below or beyond the river, and along its edge ran a narrow ledge where animals must go to drink. After he followed the rim for a couple of miles, there was a track that meandered downward, clearly the work of centuries of hooves of antelope or buffalo or other game.

It was time the horses got a bellyful of water, though he at first thought the slot was too narrow to admit the big beasts. He decided he would go down with the big water skin and bring back enough to give them a good drink. That was not an easy trip, for the cranny wiggled this way and that, though it became clear that at a pinch he might get a horse down it. Before he left here he would bring down the animals for a filling draught of water.

When he arrived at the bottom he found a small stream

of good water, but beside it was the site of a battle—or a kill? There was blood on the stone, soaked into the gritty soil, and there was clear sign of activity—someone had been dressing out an animal.

Not an Indian. Nothing he saw indicated that a native had been there.

Drag marks showed that something heavy had been dragged downstream, and he left his water skin, checked his gun, and moved cautiously toward the hidden river. Its rush grew louder as he went, and by the time it filled his ears he could see something alien lying on the bank beside a burnt-out fire. Beyond it was a crude raft, tied securely to one of the willows growing where the stream formed a small cove.

Was it? He could hardly imagine that Katharine Salcomb had made it so far and had even rafted down the Snake. Yet there lay a woman, unconscious, her color very bad, a nasty wound in her leg, in which a knife stood upright.

He holstered his gun and knelt beside her, examining her carefully. She was alive, and to his amazement the wound had not putrefied, for she had obviously cauterized it with that knife, but passed out before she could withdraw it. He had never thought any but an Indian woman would have the nerve to do such a thing.

Before doing anything else, he lifted her head and dribbled water from his canteen between her lips. She swallowed, choked, swallowed again eagerly, but her eyes didn't open.

He rebuilt her fire, using driftwood caught among the willows. Lifting her, he laid her on her crude fur blanket beside the fire. He hurried back up the ravine, all the way to his horses on the cliff top, where he unbuckled the big pack from the packhorse, hobbled the animals, and left them to graze while he returned to the wounded woman.

Once back beside his fire, he boiled water in his pot,

added meat from the store she had arranged to dry, and while the stew cooked he prepared to attend to the leg-wound. First he cleaned the entire thigh, using a clean rag from his pack, wet with river water. She flinched and moaned as he did this, but she didn't wake.

When he laid his hand on the knife, her eyes opened and she gasped with pain.

"Who?"

The word was almost inaudible.

CHAPTER TWENTY

There had been a long time of fever-dreams, Katharine knew. Those had been punctuated by pain and thirst, but the dreams had dominated her for a dark and disturbing period. She had seen her mother die, then her father. She had dreamed of avenging herself on her cousin, taking him down by battering his head with a stick of wood, then dropping rocks on him until he was entirely buried. While this had satisfied some savage element in her, it also left her feeling sick—or was that the fever?

There was nothing but pain, then, for a long while. The rush of the river became a part of her, but it did not cool the fever in her blood. That rolled down her limbs in waves of aching misery, and it made her feel as if her body wavered on the brink of a terrible fall. Amid a storm of dizziness and nausea, she realized that water was dribbling between her lips. She swallowed it and waited for more, but that did not come. Instead, a violent pain shot through her thigh around the knife, as something touched the haft.

Her question got no reply except one finger laid gently over her lips. Then a hard hand held down her leg while the other jerked the knife blade free. Katharine swallowed a scream of agony, but the pain aroused her fully. She saw a muscular arm, a hand holding the knife, a dark shoulder silhouetted against the blazing sky. There was a man there, and he had removed the knife, which had to be a good thing. He was definitely not One-Ear Murray, which was even better.

"Water," she managed to gasp. "Water?"

He turned a leather-brown face, creased by weather and laughter, toward her, and she felt immediately reassured. "I think we can spare another sip," he said. "But remember, we have to take it slow. Too much will make you sick."

Katharine nodded warily, feeling the world spin around her. When it settled again, she felt the pressure of a canteen against her mouth, and she took a cautious swallow.

"Good," the friendly voice said. "Maybe one more, while we're at it?"

The water seemed to soak into her very bones and muscles, relieving some of the terrible dryness that had made the fever worse. She let her head drop back onto the blanket and took a deep breath. Slowly, the cliffs looming over the canyon seemed to slow their circling until they stood steady against puffy clouds. She could smell something—something vile—and realized it was probably scraps of her kill that she'd had no time to clean away and bury. And that reminded her of that all-important store of meat.

"My meat? Has it rotted? I tried to make it ready to dry." Then she looked more closely at the brown face that bent over her. "Who are you?" she asked. "How did you find me?"

Sensibly, he answered the most important question first. "The meat looks fine. You did a great job of it, and only a bit the crows carried down to the ground got ruined. How in 'ell did you kill that animal, anyway? I don't see any sign you had a gun."

Again she asked, "Who are you?"

He looked rueful, a bit guilty. "I guess I'd better come clean. My name is Sun-Shot O'Neill. I'm the man that bastard Murray hired to track you down."

She tried to heave herself to a sitting position, but she was too weak and dizzy to make it. "You think you're going to take me to him? I'll kill you with my hands before I'll let you do that!" she growled.

"Lady, I know that," he said, with a hint of a chuckle. "I'd think a long time before I'd tackle you in a hand-to-hand fight. I followed you across some of the hardest country there is, and you didn't put a foot wrong. It was just bad luck that those hunters spooked your horse and made him throw you down that mountainside. And now I find you had the guts to cauterize your own wound, else I might've found you near dead with infection. I've got a lot of respect for you, believe me.

"Anyway, I'd already decided not to do what Murray hired me to do, and I might've killed him myself. But the fool took it into his head to try to grab him a woman from a bunch of Paiutes who were moving camp. You can relish the fact that they did him up brown, the whole entire program, and he was glad to die when they finally killed him." He paused and studied her face, his dark eyes curious, as if he wondered what her reaction would be.

For a moment Katharine felt a cool wash of relief that almost overcame the fever in her blood. He was dead, that gross, cruel monster who had bought her as if she were an animal. Then she remembered stories she had heard her Shoshone friends tell around the campfires, tales of captives skinned and roasted alive, suspended head-down over a fire until their brains boiled—horrible accounts of their endurance and their attitudes and words and screams while they were being entertained.

The thought sickened her. Even Murray didn't deserve such an end.

She swallowed hard and said, "I'm glad he's dead, but—that was a terrible thing, even for him. Make no mistake, if I'd had the chance I'd have killed him, but I'm not much of one for making somebody suffer." She thought for a moment. Then she added, "But it makes you wonder if Providence doesn't take a hand in things, sometimes."

O'Neill leaned back against the cliff and guffawed. At last he wiped tears of laughter from his eyes and said, "My folks would agree. They were missionaries all their working lives, and they tried to persuade the Cheyenne they preached to, to leave punishment up to the Lord; but they never did get much agreement from them. I don't think that's an idea that Indians will ever take to, or turn the other cheek, for that matter."

She almost chuckled at the thought of a lot of Pawnee or Blackfeet turning the other cheek. Then she wondered about his people. "Who are your folks? Do they live in Stony Flat?"

Seeing that talking would pass the time while his stew cooked, Sun-Shot settled onto a rock against the cliff and got comfortable. He began with his childhood among the Cheyenne; as he talked, she began to relax and her pain began to ease a bit.

By the time he reached his reason for accepting Murray's commission, the pot of stew had boiled tender, and was smelling delicious. He ended his narrative with his discovery of the site of her kill, rose to his feet and said, "Now it's time you put some food into you. Can you chew, or should I dip up some of the broth in my tin cup?"

Katharine moved her jaws, gritted her teeth, and decided that nothing bad had happened to either. "I think I'll try something chewy," she said. "I was mighty nigh starved before I tackled that antelope, and I'm even hungrier now." She realized as she spoke that her stomach felt as if it were stuck to her backbone.

Even so, she approached the tin cup of stew cautiously. Not for nothing had she helped her mother with sick people when she was a child. Eating after long abstinence could make you very ill, so she sipped the broth first, drank a few sips of water, and rested for a while before taking a bite of the meat. She chewed that for a long time, letting bits slip down her throat slowly until she had finished her ration. A faint queasiness made her lie back for a bit, but she beamed at Sun-Shot with all the gratitude in her heart.

"You may have hired on to catch me, but I think you've saved my life," she said. She burped loudly and blushed. Her belly was not used to being filled, these days, and she suspected she might have to baby it for a while.

O'Neill finished his tin pan of stew and grinned back. "Shame I ran out of coffee a while back. A cup would come in just right. But what we don't have we have to do without. I'm just grateful you had all that antelope meat. I don't think boiled jerky would have been near as good for somebody as starved as you."

He rose and covered the stew pot carefully, then tidied up her camp site, getting rid of all those fragments of bone and scrap and hide that were stinking up the place. She watched him until her eyes closed, and this time she slept peacefully, though knowing what her rescuer had set out to do should have made her too uneasy for slumber. There was something trustworthy about the fellow, she decided. And now that Murray was dead, what did she really have to worry about?

* * * * * * *

The next morning her question was answered. She woke to find herself being heaved over a shoulder, then carried up the ravine. "What?" she asked.

"River's rising," Sun-Shot grunted. "I'll put you down here—should be high enough. I'm goin' back to get all the stuff, particularly that meat. You got anything on that raft you might need?"

She almost laughed. "Everything there is something I cobbled up from driftwood, hides, and bones," she said.

"Except my knife: I've got to have that."

He reached into his belt and held the blade up. "Thought you might be a bit attached to this thing," he said. "Tie it to your belt—we've got to go up that antelope track to find my horses. I hope you're up to it." He turned back down the ravine.

Stiff and sore and still weak, Katharine stretched her limbs, groaning, and pushed herself upright. Finding her thigh extremely painful, she forced herself to stand. She could push through pain as well as anybody; years of breaking and training horses had seen to that. There hadn't been a month of her adult life when she hadn't suffered some injury that she'd learned to ignore, except for the broken leg when she was seventeen. Even that had only stopped her from her work for a few weeks.

"I'll get up that track if I have to crawl," she said aloud.

While she waited, she flexed her legs and shoulders, pushing through the misery in her thigh. She found to her relief that she seemed not to be feverish, and she thanked her mother yet again for making her assist with injuries, wounds, and illnesses. She had learned in a hard school, and it had often sickened her when she was a child, but she had no doubt that the experiences had saved her life many times since she left her home.

When she heard Sun-Shot's boots sloshing along the edge of the stream, she was standing, ready to move out. Even the short while she had waited had seen the water level rise appreciably, and she could see by the marks on the ravine walls that levels had sometimes been higher than her head. If there had been a cloudburst somewhere upstream, the river would push its excess flow into the channel of every stream running into it.

The guide came into view around the last bend carrying a large burden wrapped in her rabbit fur blanket. Everything was wet, which told her that the water levels were coming up even faster than she had thought. "I'm ready to go," she said. "The walls of the track will give me some support, so I think I can make it without any help. Seems you have your hands full without having to crutch me along."

He chuckled, shifting his load so as to make it fit through the gap into the track. "I brought you a stick I found in the drift, which should help a bit. I'll lean it against the wall and go first, so you won't feel as if you need to hurry. When I get to the top, I'll drop all this stuff and come back to help you."

He sidled into the track and began the climb to the plain above, while Katharine used the stick to help support her weight. Putting her shoulder against the side of the cut, she crept upward by stepping forward on her good leg, using the stick to relieve the weight on the other, then dragging the bad one after it. It worked out fairly well, though after every two steps she had to lean hard on the wall and recoup her strength. That made it a very long trip, though she had made it in a few minutes when scouting out the game.

Before she made it halfway, O'Neill came back to meet her, and his arm taking the pressure off her bad leg helped incredibly. He half-carried her the rest of the way up the cut and set her onto the sun-crisped grass of the plain beside the gear he had dumped there. Katharine sat upright and looked around her, trying to ignore the misery in her leg.

It must be late August by now, she guessed, or maybe even early September. She had been so engrossed in surviving her grueling journey that it hadn't occurred to her to count days. In any case, she could tell by the angle of the sun that the year was beginning to wane.

A familiar sound brought her head around—two horses were munching the dried grass, a few yards away. Though they were hobbled, she could see that these were well cared for, satisfied with their condition, and in no mood to run away. As an experienced horse trainer, she diagnosed their expressions to be as smug as horse faces could look. If she had not already judged O'Neill to be a kind person, this would have done the job. A man might fool people on a consistent basis, but nobody ever deceived a horse he lived and worked with every day. She had judged Murray by the demeanor of the mounts he rode, all of which looked dejected, not to mention skinny, and that had been an accurate assessment.

She rolled over onto all-fours and began to struggle to her feet. This late in the year, she needed to find a place to spend the winter, for, injured as she was, there was no way she could hurry enough to beat the snows to the mountains she must cross to reach her aunt in western Oregon. That meant she must ask O'Neill to help her reach some kind of refuge before he turned back toward his home and his parents. The thought rankled her independent nature, but she had learned practicality in a hard school, and she stiffened her resolve. This was something she must do.

After taking them down to water and leading them up the track again, O'Neill had been packing the horses, dividing the pack animal's burden with his own Goldie, and setting the bits back in their mouths. He turned to her, and his eyes widened as he realized she was standing, albeit somewhat unsteadily. "Can you ride?" he asked, leading Goldie toward her.

She examined the horse, then looked at the other, which had no saddle, only the pack frame. "I think I will be able to ride, but a stirrup is going to put too much pressure on the leg. I think I can manage better using the pack frame like a sort of sidesaddle, resting the bad one along it, instead of letting it hang or putting weight on it, if you use the old fur blanket to pad my seat. I dunno how long I can hang on, but if you'll help me get to someplace where I can survive the winter, I'll be eternally grateful. I simply don't see how I'd be able to go fast enough to beat the snow in the high country."

Sun-Shot took her words in order of importance. "I think you're right about the frame. I can rig a sort of sling you can slip your ankle through to keep the pressure off it. Good thinkin'." Then he grinned at her, his hands already busy with rope to form the sling. "As for findin' you good winter quarters, if you knew me better you'd know that my parents didn't raise me to leave an injured person alone to face the winter in this country. They'd disown me if I got back to Stony Flat and told 'em I'd left a young lady to fend for herself like that." He folded the blanket several times and secured it to serve as a sort of saddle pad.

Katharine grinned back at him. She had already drawn that conclusion for herself. "Then I'll put myself into your expert hands and follow your advice, whatever it takes. It isn't going to be...easy." She reached up to grab the pack frame as he halted the horse beside her.

As she heaved herself upward, he boosted her, taking the strain off her shoulders and the good leg. She set her foot into the loop that he had made to serve as a stirrup and groaned as she forced the injured leg up in order to put her other foot through that useful sling. Once she got herself settled in place, she found the position less painful than she expected.

Looking down at the guide, she nodded. "I don't know for how long, but I think I can do this for a reasonable time. Let's go and try it out, anyway. This is a hell of a lot better than steering a driftwood raft down the Snake, I can testify to that."

CHAPTER TWENTY-ONE

By the time they got underway, the sun was high, and a brisk wind was blowing out of the northwest. After chasing his hat for a quarter of a mile, Sun-Shot tied it down with his bandana and settled himself for a long day in the saddle. The horses had taken a long rest, the grass, while dry, had been abundant, and before leaving the stream he had watered both generously, as well as filling his water skins and canteens. They stepped out energetically and traveled without words for several hours.

"What's his name?"

The question caught him unprepared, and he turned in the saddle to look back at the girl. She pointed down at her mount. "I hate riding a beast without a name, and if you haven't given him one, I'm going to," she said.

O'Neill dropped back to ride beside her. "Well, Murray had a name for him, but it's one my folks taught me not to speak, and I certainly wouldn't repeat it to a lady. I guess you'd better come up with one of your own. I just called him Horse." He found himself holding back a laugh. What was there about this strange woman that tickled him so much?

She nodded. "Then I'll name him Crowfoot," she said. She must have read the puzzlement on his face, for she added, "I used to have a gelding that looked like him. His name was Crowfoot, too. Good horse—I hope this one is as good."

He could identify with that. This was his third, no, his fourth Goldie. A good horse was something you wanted to hang onto, if only through its name. Then Goldie's ears flicked upward, and he whickered.

"Whoa," Sun-Shot said softly, and without a word Katharine reined Crowfoot in and waited.

O'Neill dismounted and handed his reins to the girl. "There's something up ahead, and out here anything you don't know about is automatically dangerous. I'm goin' to stroll up a ways until I can see what Goldie senses. If there's nothing to worry about, I'll signal, and you can bring the horses up. But if I wave you off, you ride like hell, you understand?"

She took the reins and turned Crowfoot toward the shelter of a pile of rounded boulders formed by some ancient flooding of the Snake; it was not a great hiding place but better than sticking up clearly on the flat ground. "I'll watch you like a hawk."

He started away, then turned back. "There's a spare revolver in my pack. Pull Goldie over and find it, along with the bag of cartridges. If something should...happen... to me, you'll need a gun."

"Don't think you're going to get away that easily," she said. "If you run into trouble I'll take that pistol and come to the rescue. Turnabout is only fair play, you know."

The little devil would do it, too, he knew. That meant he had to be even more cautious than usual.

* * * * * * *

Before he had gone a half-mile, Sun-Shot felt a change in the air. Instead of the normal desert atmosphere, he felt an uneasy tingle as irregular gusts of wind replaced the former steady flow. He felt a quiver of apprehension as he rose onto his toes and stared toward the northwest. Instead of the sun-gilded glare that had blasted the plain for many days, on the horizon there was a darkness in the sky that extended like a vast curtain to the ground, a black pall that was moving toward him too fast for comfort

He turned and ran toward the distant cluster of rocks that marked the position of Katharine and the horses. Poor as it was, that formed the only possible shelter within eyeshot, and he knew there was no time to search for better cover. By the time he reached the spot, Katharine had seen the approaching storm and had managed, somehow, to dismount and secure the horses, using rope from the pack that she looped around one of the biggest stones. She then rolled the chunk of rock over onto the line.

Grit was now pelting them, and dust was beginning to make breathing difficult, for the storm was upon them. He pushed Katharine into a sort of notch where the melon-shaped rocks had formed a shallow opening. Then he lurched through the wind and sand to the horses, pulled the packs off their backs and shoved those into the cranny with the girl. The horses had their rumps to the wind, their heads down, and he knew they would endure whatever came. Unfortunately he had learned firsthand that people's skin was not as tough as horsehide.

He returned to the scanty shelter and pushed in beside Katharine. He motioned to her to use one pack to shield her head, while he used the other. "Cover your nose and mouth!" he yelled above the clamor of the wind. He pulled an edge of one blanket free of his pack and saw her doing the same with the other. Then they burrowed, ostrich-like, into their makeshift protections, which were anchored by the weight of the packs, and he prepared to tough out the storm.

His clothing whipped about him, almost skinning him at times. Fine dust filled the tiny tent over his head, and he found himself gasping for air, while he held himself to the ground by wedging himself against the boulders, when gusts tried to tumble him away over the desert.

The trial seemed to last forever. When the wind had diminished to a point at which he thought he could stand against it, he began to move. Lifting the blanket, which was weighted with enough sand to bury a body, he heaved himself to a sitting position and found himself watching an adjacent sand pile do the same.

He opened his mouth, tried to speak, choked, and began to cough. His companion was doing the same, and they sat side by side, amid the last whirls and blasts of the storm, trying to clear their noses and eyes and lungs of the clogging dust.

At last Katharine blew her nose between her fingers, lacking any sort of handkerchief. "Bad enough," she grunted. "Could have been Indians." She hawked and spat.

Sun-Shot chuckled and choked. "I agree," he said. "A bunch of angry Shoshone or Paiute or Blackfoot would have really added pepper to the vinegar." He rose to his feet, feeling sand even inside his boots, sat on a rock and emptied both. He could have started a pretty good rock garden with the gritty soil inside them.

Katharine had shaken the dust from her blanket and was trying to comb sand from her hair with her fingers. Her face was tan-gray with layered dust, and Sun-Shot knew his own was no better. If her throat was as dry as his, they both needed water; he pulled one of the water skins out of the pile of rocks and handed it to her. She took it gratefully and drank deeply, before handing it back to him. It was heavy, for it was almost full, and after he drank he pulled his small iron pot from the pack and filled it with water.

The horses snorted and stamped, smelling the water, and they gulped it greedily. Thank goodness he had filled up at the river. It was a good two-day trip to cut across this loop, and by the time they came to the Snake again they would be running pretty short. A horse could consume many gallons of water a day, even in less arid country than this. Carrying enough for their extended needs was almost impossible.

Nevertheless, he and Katharine used a bit of the precious liquid to clean their eyes and dab most of the dust off their faces. Sun-Shot felt a bit more human after that, as he tightened the packs, reloaded the horses, and gave the girl a boost onto her horse. Late though it was, he wanted to travel a good few miles before darkness fell. Looking up into Katharine's eyes, he saw agreement there.

The storm had left the sky clear, but with the sun dropping in the west the heat was much less. The horses, having snorted the dust from their nostrils and flapped it from their ears, seemed anxious to go, too, and they stepped along at a ground-eating pace.

"Have you been this way before?" Katharine's question caught him by surprise, for Sun-Shot was deep in thought regarding a good place to camp for the night.

"I guided some wagon trains this way, before the War started," he said. "When you do that, you scout out all the land roundabout, checking for hostiles, finding good campsites, and locating sources of grass and fuel. That was before the settlers' cattle began trampling down the plants the Paiute eat and scaring away the antelope and buffalo. Just before the War began the Indians just plain got worn out with putting up with that and began being hostile.

"If that hadn't happened, I could've found you a good winter place with one of the clans. Now I'm goin' to have to locate somethin' else. But I know where to look. The Salmon River, up a ways, has some nice little valleys along its course, and if I'm not mistaken some whites will have claimed one or two and set up farms or ranches."

She grunted, instead of replying. Glancing around, he could see that already her leg was giving her trouble. He'd suffered similar discomfort in his time, and he knew she was ignoring the misery, focusing on the plain around them and the hills rising on the horizon.

He slowed Goldie's pace, knowing that would ease the jarring of her wounded thigh. If he remembered correctly, they might reach his goal before night, and surely some thrifty ranching family would have settled there and begun ranching. In this sparsely inhabited country, that was the best refuge he could think of in which his charge might spend the winter.

CHAPTER TWENTY-TWO

Katharine felt that she had been caught up in some sort of tornado over the past days. Now, for the first time since leaving Sand Flat, she had time to think, and in order to escape the discomfort in her leg she sank into her thoughts, re-creating the strange sequence of events since she killed the antelope.

She had expected to die of the stab in her thigh, and her effort with the red-hot knife blade had merely been her determination not to give up without trying her best. According to Sun-Shot, that had saved her life. He had insisted that he only fed her a bit and carried her away from the flooding river. But she knew better.

She had been on the verge of starvation when she attempted the kill, using the last of her strength for that last desperate attempt to survive. Her long experience helping her mother with human ailments had told her, long before she reached that point, that she was on her last legs. When her monthly period stopped, early in her journey, she had understood she was using up her reserves of flesh and strength in a dangerous manner. If she lived now it would be due to the man who had been hired to catch her and take her back into slavery. Her father would have appreciated the irony of that, she thought, though if he had lived, her cousin would never have dared to try selling her.

Crowfoot snorted, bringing her out of her thoughts to a fresh awareness of her thigh. It was definitely getting better, for Sun-Shot had used some Cheyenne remedy he carried with him in a small horn container. Though it smelled vile, it seemed to work well, and she knew she was on the mend.

Her guide insisted upon stopping to cook more of the antelope at regular intervals. "You went too long on too little food. Now we've got to build your strength pretty fast. Whatever happens, you're goin' to need it. Winter is a hard thing to handle, even if you hadn't anything else to worry about."

She knew he was right. There was no way she could travel fast enough to reach her aunt in Oregon, for already the distant mountains to the east were touched with snow. Without a guide, it would take her far longer than normal to make the journey, even in summer. Whatever refuge O'Neill might locate for her, she would not consent to burden others with her keep. She would work at something and pull her own weight, if it killed her.

Knowing that, she never objected to her frequent meals, though often she felt somewhat queasy after eating. Her stomach, so long deprived, was having a hard time adjusting to the new state of affairs. She could tell that she was getting stronger, though it had been only a few days since O'Neill had found her. She wondered about that. Ranch work had made her tough and strong. Her journey had taught her even more difficult lessons. But she felt that she had inherited a stubborn determination not to quit from both her parents, and she felt that might be the most valuable element of all.

There was plenty to take her mind off the ache down her leg, as she followed Goldie over the sagebrush-studded plain and into the edges of the dry brown hills. "The river's not far now. Another day and we should find the canyon. Even now, there should be somebody farming one of those little valleys. Might be old folks or young fellows who don't like the War," O'Neill murmured.

As they plodded along, saving the horses, Katharine considered what he said. She had no enthusiasm for spending a winter with any young man who was living by himself, for she had no intention of repeating her recent problem with Murray. As for old people—well, if she thought she could be of help to them, maybe, but if not she wouldn't be beholden to them.

By nightfall O'Neill assured her that tomorrow would see them at the river he sought. Katharine was so tired she hardly paid attention, just ate and rolled herself in her blanket, grateful that One-Ear had left his extra supplies on the pack horse instead of taking it with him on his stupid and fatal foray. She slept hard, without dreaming, and when her companion nudged her shoulder to wake her, she knew that she had passed the mark and was well on her way to being well again.

She rose and helped pack the horses, finding that she could get around without favoring the leg too much. As the sun mounted above the dust-colored mountains, she climbed onto Crowfoot without help and knew that she would be in shape to make a decision about her future, when the time came.

Sun-Shot led off around a low ridge, down a slope, then up a sharper one. When they reached the crest of that, she could see the ragged wall of a canyon below.

O'Neill turned back and asked, "You think you can walk a bit? From here down it's best not to try riding. The path's too narrow; your weight could overbalance your mount and take you both down."

She nodded. "I'm a lot stronger now, and the leg isn't too bad. I sure could use a walking stick, though."

He cocked his head, grunted, and slid off Goldie. "Be right back."

He was. In a few minutes he reappeared around the sharp bend in the path and handed her a stout branch, evidently cut from a cottonwood. "The water's not all that far down, when you don't have to worry about horses. You take that. Let me go first, so if you trip I'll be there for you to fall on. The horses will follow us; they know there's water down there and you couldn't keep them from it if you tried."

The plan worked fairly well, though she found it hard to keep her footing, even with the stick, as the leg had not regained its strength. They made it down at last, however, and found themselves on a flat shelf of rocky soil some yards above a narrow channel whose water existed more as a chain of puddles than as a real stream. Small cottonwoods thrust their tops above the level of the track, and Katharine saw the broken branch that had supplied her stick. As they descended to the water level, she realized that willows also grew there.

The soil there was dry and gritty, for it was, after all, the driest part of the year. Yet she could see that with water and care it might nurture grass and even a vegetable garden. Beyond the stream bed was an even larger patch of land, and Katharine could see that one of those might provide enough space for a house and grazing for cattle or horses. Protected on either hand by the cliffs forming the ravine, such a location could be considered a good one, if you didn't have too much ambition. You could use adjacent strips of arable land along the stream to create a ranch of whatever size you had the energy to work.

They stopped to rest themselves and their mounts, using bits of dry cottonwood to build a fire for another of those too-frequent meals. Sitting on a lip of stone, she grinned at Sun-Shot. "You seem to have found what you were looking for, Mr. O'Neill. Now can you conjure up a suitable winter home for a young lady?"

His weathered face crinkled with his own smile. "If it's not suitable, I'll take you home to my parents. They'd be glad to have you; they need somebody to look after them, and I'm gone so much I can't do that. I'd planned to go back by way of Fort Hall to see if I could pick up some scout work, but my folks would disown me if I left you someplace where you wouldn't be safe."

Katharine had learned enough about the man, as they traveled together, to know that arguing would be useless. When the time came she would make her own decision. She had traveled long past any patience with having others plan her life.

CHAPTER TWENTY-THREE

As they traveled along the river, Sun-Shot kept a sharp eye out for animal tracks, for the antelope meat was a thing of the past, and for days they had been living on his supply of jerky and canned beans. At this time of year the small creatures kept close to a water supply, and he saw many tracks of rabbits and badgers and ground squirrels. Then, rounding a groin of stone that thrust out from the canyon wall, he saw a cow path ending at the river and leading back up the canyon into a cut in the cliff. The tracks of several cows marked the trail, and partially dried dung showed that it had not been long since they visited their drinking place.

He could also see where those sharp double-pointed hooves had trampled the plants along the waterside and the drier growths where they had grazed. It was this, more than anything, that had angered the tribes in this arid country, for their food supply depended upon all kinds of plants, roots, herbs, and seeds, as well as game. For most, meat was not a regular staple of their diets, while gleanings from the land formed the bulk of the food supply. He could understand their fury and distress, but that would not stop his own kind from moving outward from the populated centers in the east to take what they wanted from people they considered nothing more than animals. It saddened him to think that people who considered themselves civilized could justify their depredations in such a way.

He sighed and remounted Goldie to follow the trail. Though cows were great sources of meat, a whole animal was too much for only two people who had no dependable way of preserving it quickly. Besides, if he was not mistaken, these animals belonged to someone living upstream. It wasn't advisable to begin an acquaintance by butchering someone else's beast. People on the frontier were notoriously fierce in defending their property. For that matter, he was himself.

Katharine's voice came from behind him. "You think someone lives up there where the cow path goes? Or are these wild cattle or buffalo? Though the tracks seem small for buffalo."

He should have known a ranch girl would spot such traces. She was too quick by half, he had decided long ago. He turned in the saddle and said, "We'll see pretty soon. These little valleys are so small we'll cross them fast, and sooner or later we'll come up with that herd. I expect we'll find a settler, too."

They found a house of sorts in the third of the small grass patches. Backed against the canyon wall, it was formed of cottonwood logs and stone. It had a mud chimney, from which a trickle of smoke oozed. A smudge of fire also burned in the small yard, its smoke carried away up the canyon by the wind that funneled along the river.

Sun-Shot raised his hand, and both horses halted. "Hayooooh!" he yelled. "Anybody home?"

His words echoed eerily around the complex of irregular walls surrounding the small homestead. A distant bawl told him that the herd was within earshot and was probably used to being handled by human beings.

He dismounted and helped Katharine down from Crowfoot, for he could see that the leg had stiffened too much for her to remove it from the sling. He helped her free it and then lifted her off the horse. She grunted when her feet hit the ground, but she refused to lean on him as she limped toward the fire.

He eased the gear on the horses, freed the bits so they could graze easily and drink from the stream. "There's got to be somebody nearby or they wouldn't have left the fire unattended," he called after her. "Nobody out here minds if travelers use their fire. Sit down on that rock and rest your leg, why don't you?"

She nodded and sank onto a flat boulder near the fire; it was obviously used as a table, a seat, or a work space, whatever was needed. The year was now far enough along so that there was a chill in the air, and the wind made her shiver. She could use that fire, he thought, as he made his way forward to join her.

He dropped one of the packs at her feet and dug out a heavy woolen shirt his mother had insisted he take with him on every expedition. It always made him itch, but he faithfully carried it with him wherever he went. Now he was glad, for when he put it around the girl's shoulders she snuggled into it gratefully.

Then they both froze in place, for a sound reached their ears, a faint groan, barely audible above the rustle of the wind in the cottonwoods and willows. Sun-Shot turned to look into her face, and she nodded. He pulled her to stand beside him, and they moved quickly toward the narrow porch that was made of flat stones from the river.

The door was made of layers of cowhide, stretched over a willow frame. He pushed against it, and it swung open on leather hinges, revealing a fairly large room, dark because of the lack of windows. The crude hearth showed a glimmer of coals, though it did not give enough light to see by. Now the groan sounded again, louder than before. Sun-Shot moved forward cautiously, wary of stumbling over something on the cluttered floor. Still, he stepped on something hard, eliciting a yelp of pain.

The largest lump was a person rolled in blankets, he found by feeling it over. He could hear Katharine fumbling about across the room. Then she knelt beside the hearth, and he knew she was using the live coals for fire. A lamp flared into life, and he could see the old man in the blankets. He was almost blue with cold, and his breathing was ragged.

"We've got to get this fellow warm," he said. "Else he's goin' to check out on us. Wonder where his folks are—that fire hasn't been doin' him much good, burnt out like it is."

"I'll find the woodpile," the girl said. "You move him as close to the hearth as you can, and we can maybe warm him up enough to keep him alive." Carrying the lamp, she searched the corners of the room, and he could see a small stack of wood against the back wall.

Before he could lift the sick man and move him, Katharine had arranged sticks of split wood on the coals and had blown them into a blaze. Sputtering and crackling, the fire blossomed, and Sun-Shot laid the bundle of blankets close. Then, with Katharine's help, he peeled back the coverings and chafed the man's wrists, rubbed his chest, and turned him so that the warmth could reach his skin.

As soon as he seemed to be breathing better, the girl rose to her feet and caught up a pot sitting beside the fireplace. "I'll fill this with water and heat it. If we can get something hot into him, that should help. Broth would probably work, though I do wish we had some coffee. Be right back!" Then she limped away through the cowhide door.

Sun-Shot grinned down at the fellow on the floor. He was beginning to look better, though his breath still came through terrible congestion. "That one will do to ride the river with," he said to the unconscious man.

Now the fire was lighting the windowless room enough to let him see, and he rose and looked around for a candle or something of the sort. He found a dish of tallow with a strand of rag in it, the crudest sort of lamp, and he wondered where the other lamp had come from. Maybe something brought painfully across the mountains from home in the east, he thought, as he lit the wick with a splinter kindled in the fire. The smell was strong, but it gave a flickering yellow light that allowed him to look around for food in the cabin.

Dug into the wall against the cliff he found a stash of canned stuff, beans and peaches, mainly. This had been a person who provided for the future, it was clear. But the sweet juice from the peaches might be of help, giving the sick man something to strengthen him. The cans were cold to his touch, however, and he knew it would be better to get hot liquid into the sufferer and save the sweet stuff for later.

Katharine's steps sounded on the stone outside, and she pushed aside the door. She set the pot in the edge of the coals to heat, dropped in strips of jerky, and returned to check on their patient.

She felt his forehead, set her fingers on the pulse in his neck, and examined the color of his skin. "He looks a bit better," she murmured. "The fire is helping, and when we have some hot broth to give him he should improve even more. "

Sun-Shot regarded her with interest. "You sound like you know what you're doing," he said.

She glanced up to meet his gaze. "I should know. I nursed my father for two years, while he died very slowly of heart and lung trouble. Besides, my mother was a healer, and I got extra teaching from our Shoshone friends. I think this fellow can make it, if we can get him warm and build up his strength. He's pretty far gone, though, and it will take close attention for a good while."

She looked around the untidy room and grunted. "I take it there's no woman here to nurse him. I wonder who built that fire in the yard."

That was a question that was not answered until almost

dark, when someone outside yelled, "Who's in our house? Pap, are you all right? Whoever you are, come out so I can see you. I warn you, I got a gun!"

"Let me," said Katharine. "I don't look threatening."

Sun-Shot nodded, choking back a laugh. He suspected that, inch for inch, this young woman was even more dangerous than he was.

Nevertheless, he crept to the doorway and opened a slit through which to peer. In the small yard Katharine was standing erect, facing a skinny youngster holding a rifle almost as long as he was. He was dressed in buckskin leggings and a calico shirt that looked as if it had begun life as part of a woman's dress. His hair was long and black, bound around his head, Indian-style, with a strip of leather. "What you doin' here?" he asked, his voice rising to a squeak. "Who be, you, anyway?"

"My name is Katharine Salcomb," she said, moving toward him gently, her hand out. "Is that your father in the house? He is very sick. We built up the fire, and I have a pot of water simmering to boil him some jerky broth. Was he sick when you left?"

Her tone was so easy and natural, her appearance so non-threatening that the boy handed her the rifle. "That's my Pap, but he wasn't all that sick when I went up to take the horses to fresh grazing. He felt poorly, but I left him a good fire and plenty of wood in the house."

"I know," she said, setting the rifle on the big rock. "The fire was just about out, and he was cold as death, but we're warming him up. Can you gather me a bunch of willow bark from the creek over there? I'll make him some tea with that, in case he gets feverish."

The boy said, "I'll go get the willow, but I want to see Pap first." She nodded, and he ran into the house.

He slowed when he saw Sun-Shot pulling back the door, but he came forward to kneel beside the pallet where his father lay. The guide heard him swallow hard as he saw how sick the man truly was. "You think he'll be all right?" the boy asked.

"If we can manage it, he will. By the bye, what's your name, Son?"

"Makopi, my mother called me, though my Pap calls me Mak. His name is Elton Frazier."

"Your mother was what? Shoshone? "

"My mother was Hidatsa. My Pap brought her with him from beyond the mountains. She died two winters ago of the coughing sickness." Mak looked sad, and Sun-Dance nodded with understanding.

"This is a good place," Sun-Shot said. "Plenty of grass, even in fall. Your cattle must be fat."

Mak's eyes grew bright. "Our cattle are fat, and our horses are strong. I just came from putting them in their winter place. In summer they graze out on the plains, but when snow comes to the mountaintops we bring them down into the canyons, sheltered from the blizzards and close to waters that never freeze."

The boy rose from his knees and said, "I will go and bring willow bark, as the woman said. She is a healer?"

"The best one I know anywhere in this part of the country," he said, and that was no lie. She seemed to know what was best to do, that was certain.

By nightfall, Katharine had managed to get two cupfuls of broth into Frazier. He came to enough to recognize his son, who had brought enough willow bark to dose everyone in the area. Then Katharine persuaded him to drink a bit of the peach syrup, and he fell asleep suddenly and deeply.

The boy spread his blanket beside his father, and Sun-Shot and Katharine found space for theirs along the farther wall. The fire was banked so as to smolder slowly without going out entirely, and from time to time the guide or the girl would rise to add fuel. There was no use in allowing Frazier to chill again.

By morning the boy had lost any wariness he had shown for the two strangers, and his father showed some improvement. Sun-Shot regarded the man with some concern. He was obviously very ill, and medical treatment, other than tending to wounds, was not one of his skills. He turned to Katharine, his eyebrows raised.

She folded her blanket neatly, did the same for his, and gestured for him to follow her outside. Aloud, she said, "We need to get fresh water. I want you to help me with something, as well."

"What's this about?" he asked her, once they were beyond earshot of the boy.

"He's very sick," she said. "I think he has a lung congestion, and I listened to his heart in the night. We need to build a sweat lodge and get him very warm. I wish I had some hawthorn berry—Mama had a store she used to trade for with women headed west who were taking their remedies with them. But no use thinking about things we can't get."

Glancing around the flat area holding the cabin, she asked, "Does mullein grow around here?"

Sun-Shot studied the ground, the grass, the verge of the river. "Might find some upstream. You think it'll help?"

"First we need to make the sweat lodge. We can use some of those cowhides nailed to the wall of the cabin. There's plenty of wood—I see dead cottonwoods and willows, there along the river and the creek that runs up the little canyon. If we can get him warm all the way through, I think he'll have a chance. Then if we can burn mullein so he can breathe the smoke, that should clear his breathing."

He nodded. He liked someone who knew what she was doing, and it sounded as if Katharine filled the bill. "Let's get busy," he said.

CHAPTER TWENTY-FOUR

Katharine did not feel as confident as she tried to look, while she supervised the removal of her patient to the sweat lodge. There was no lack of rocks to heat in the fire, and certainly no lack of water. She filled the bucket several times as they kept the small space full of steam. Stripped to a loincloth, Frazier seemed to regain some color, as sweat streamed from his skin. The racking coughs, which had begun as soon as he awoke, lessened in intensity.

Leaving Sun-Shot and the boy to dash water onto the rocks, she went into the cabin and set the big iron pot to boiling. The boy had brought a chunk of beef into the house, along with a handful of peppers and dried squash. "My mother was a great gardener," he told her. "She taught me good, and Pap and I keep growin' stuff every year."

"I'll bet you have a lot of food stored for winter," she said.

"There's a deep cave, back up the canyon, where it stays cool even in summer. We keep our meat there, and pumpkins and squash and all sorts of stuff. I'll bring you more when you need it." He sniffed appreciatively. "That smells mighty good."

"When your Pap is warm down to his bones, and his cough has cleared up some more, this stew should be done. Then we'll all eat."

Mak returned to tending the fire in the sweat-lodge, and Katharine thought about him and his father, as she stirred the stew and made bread with the cornmeal she found in a barrel in a corner. Flattening it into palm-sized cakes, she baked it in a Dutch oven, finding herself impressed by the completeness of the Fraziers' household arrangements. Mak's Hidatsa mother must have been a good manager, she thought, for usually men didn't think of things that would make cooking easier.

She considered a lot of matters, while tending the cooking and waiting for her patient to return. By the time that happened, she had decided what was best to do.

* * * * * * *

When the men brought Frazier back into the house, wrapped in a blanket and glowing with heat, the stew was ready, the hot cornpone steaming. Though there was no table, she had found tin spoons, and the four of them sat on stools around the pot and ate ravenously.

Although talking seemed to make him cough worse, Frazier whispered, "I'd of died, Ma'am, iffen you an' your man hadn't come along. Mak's a good boy, but he had to go tend the horses, an' I got sick after he left."

"Don't talk, Mr. Frazier; that makes you worse. We're glad we happened along. But I've got to tell you, Sun-Shot isn't my husband. He is my...guide." she glanced up at O'Neill, and he nodded his agreement.

"I've had a lot of experience at nursing sick people. Besides that, I'm a first-rate horse trainer. As Sun-Shot has to get back to his folks to make sure they're fixed for the winter, I wonder if I might stay here and take care of you two over the winter? I don't want to go back east, and next summer I'll be going on to Oregon. If that's agreeable to you, I would like to stay here and take care of both of you."

She turned to Sun-Shot. "I know you've been concerned about me, when you have to go. Does this satisfy you? I think these are nice people, and I could be useful to them. Besides, there are horses to train, if they'll let me."

He grinned at Mak and his father. "She has a reputation for being as good a horse trainer as any in the Territories," he said. "Let's think this over, see if you have supplies enough, maybe do some hunting to make sure you do. If everything checks out right, that seems like a fine plan to me."

Elton Frazier agreed. "I'm gettin' old," he admitted, "and this ain't the first spell of sickness I've had. Should Miss Katharine be willin' to stay the winter, it would be a comfort to me. I worry about my boy, y'know. He's a good young'un, but he's only just thirteen. We teached him good, his Ma and me, but he's awful young. Come spring, if she wants to head out west agin, things'll be better for her and us both."

Sun-Shot nodded, and Katharine smiled. This would work, she thought.

* * * * * * *

It didn't take long for the guide to satisfy himself that all was well found for the winter. He checked on the horses, now pastured in an array of branching canyons. "You'll have plenty of work, until it gets too cold," he said to Katharine. "By the time you're through, if all I hear is true, the Fraziers'll have a valuable string of mounts to sell to anyone who needs them.

"I'll leave the pack-horse for you, but I suspect when you leave Elton will insist you take the best of the ones you train." He stroked his chin and looked at her. "But I'll be thinkin' about you all the time I move toward home. Not many ladies could do what you've done, and I'm sort of...."—he blushed even through his deep tan—"...took with you."

The girl felt herself go pink, as well. "I like you a lot, Sun-Shot. But I'm not ready to pair off with anybody, right now. It'll take me a while to get over my feelings about being sold. Maybe later—if there is a later."

Two days after that, she thought about those words as she watched him ride out of sight toward the trail Mak told him would take him up onto the plain. She knew he would make it back to Sand Flat, for he would travel much faster alone. She knew he would attend to his parents' needs, because that was the kind of man he was.

She knew, as well, that she would see him again. Perhaps before she left in the spring. Perhaps in Oregon. But until then she would go her own way and do what she had planned to do, without waiting for anybody or anything.

Because that was the kind of woman she was.

www.ingramcontent.com/pod-product-compliance
Lightning Source LLC
Chambersburg PA
CBHW032011240626

47153CB00003B/1211